EVERYONE
WORTH KNOWING

EVERYONE WORTH KNOWING

SHORT STORIES

JEFF RICHARDS

CIRCUIT BREAKER BOOKS

Circuit Breaker Books LLC
Portland, OR
www.circuitbreakerbooks.com

Cover and book design by Vinnie Kinsella

ISBN: 978-1-953639-06-6
eISBN: 978-1-953639-07-3
LCCN: 2021903109

To Connie, Hannah, Baird, Ben, and Jane
With love and affection

To be blind is not miserable; not to be able to bear blindness, that is miserable.

—JOHN MILTON

Contents

Riding The Fences

WHEN FARRIS KAISER WAS TWELVE YEARS OLD, TIM NEWTON, his best friend, called him a "fairy." He smashed Tim in the mouth. Tim touched his mouth and gazed at the blood in his hand. He charged his tormentor. Farris stepped aside and slugged his friend in the back of the head. Tim went down like a sack of cement. He didn't get up. A teacher came by.

"What happened?" she asked.

"He called me a fairy," explained Farris.

When he reached home, his father asked him to cut a switch from one of the willow trees by the driveway.

"Lean against the house with your back to me," he said after Farris gave him the switch.

It was summer and he was in shorts, so he didn't have to roll up his pants like he did in the winter when he got switched. He'd been a terror since he was young, so the switching came often, but this time he wasn't going to take it. After a few stinging lashes on his calves, he whipped around, grabbed the switch, and started using it on his dad.

"You want to be a big boy, huh," said his dad, throwing a punch at his son. Farris ducked, but the second one caught him on the chin and sent him sprawling to the ground. His mother ran out to the back porch.

"Stop that, Edgar," she said.

"This boy beat up his best friend. Now it's my turn to teach him a lesson," said the old man as he reached down to grab Farris. But the boy knocked his father's hands aside, jumped up, and ran for his bike.

He pedaled his bike down the dirt driveway, past the willow trees on either side of the front gate, until he came to the dirt road. He pedaled down the road to where it ended at the base of Elk Mountain. He hid the bike behind a tree and followed a trail for a mile, then into the underbrush until he came to the creek. About a quarter mile down the creek, he came to the cascades. He removed his shoes and most of his clothes except for his underpants, tiptoed carefully across the cascade because it was slippery with moss, sat down, and slid to a pool that was five feet deep, up to his neck. Cold and refreshing. He splashed around the pool for a while and thought that he wanted to be dead. All he had to do was stick his head under the water until he could no longer breathe. Not many people came here, so he supposed it would take them a couple of days to find him floating on his stomach in his underwear. He climbed out of the pool and lay on his back. Looking high up on the ridge of Elk Mountain, he spied a hawk gliding this way and that in the thermals. He turned his head when he heard a knocking noise. It was a redheaded woodpecker hammering on a dead tree. A bunny crept out from behind a rock and stared at him. He decided that he didn't want to die, that what he actually wanted was to be as free as all the creatures in the woods.

Later that night after his dad had gone to bed, he told his mom what he thought about up in the woods.

"Son, you may think you want to be free," she said, mussing his hair. He jumped away. He didn't like to be touched. "But you're riding the fences."

She had this funny way of talking because she grew up on a ranch in Kansas.

"Your daddy's the same way. Maybe all men are that way. That's why you need women," she said, smiling at him and mussing his hair again. "We're going to tame that wild streak out of you. That's what I did with your dad, and that's what I'll do with you."

Twenty years later he has only one friend in the world, Tim Newton. They both own shiny black Indian Motorcycles and tool as far down as Dollywood, where they ride the roller coaster and camp out in the Smoky Mountains.

One day Farris wanders in a Walmart without a mask on, and a burly man with a blue vest and ponytail accosts him. Farris pushes Mr. Blue into the shopping carts and steers straight for the auto services section, where he's accosted by another bluecoat, this one much smaller in stature and wearing glasses. He knocks Four Eyes over onto a display case and notices six other bluecoats converging on him. He decides to hightail it. Before the sliding doors close behind him, he turns to offer his pursuers a digital salute. He speeds out of the parking lot in his shiny Indian and up the highway about ten miles toward home. His dad died five years ago, and he lives at home with his mom; his sister; her husband, Hank; and their kid. Hank and Sarah work the farm, and Farris helps out when it comes time to pick the apples, but mostly he works as a surveyor at a local engineering firm.

Farris lives in a converted storage shed near the main house. When he pulls up on his cycle all pissed off at Walmart—all he wanted was engine oil for his bike—Tim is sitting at his desk hunched over the computer.

"Look at this." He points at a comment on Facebook underneath the photo of a fat-faced goateed shock jock:

MASKS ARE A PSYCHOLOGICAL WEAPON TO
LIMIT OUR FREEDOM.
WHEN YOU WEAR A MASK YOU ARE DECLARING
THAT ALL HUMANS
ARE DANGEROUS, INFECTIOUS, AND THREATS.
YOU ARE NO LONGER IN CHARGE OF YOUR LIFE.

"Isn't that the truth," says Farris, looking more carefully at the screen. He doesn't know about the rest of it, but he agrees with the last sentence of the comment. He wasn't going to let anyone mess with his life. He tells Tim what happened at Walmart.

Tim pokes him in the shoulder. "Way to go, man," he says. Ever since that long-ago fight, Tim's been totally under his spell. When Farris purchased his Indian bike, Tim zoomed up the driveway a week later with a precise clone. It's enough to give Farris the jitters. But what choice does he have? Both he and Tim have been antsy the last couple of weeks. Since the pandemic moved into the valley, business has slackened at the engineering firm, and he has little to do other than putter around the farm.

"Hey, man, you know what?" declares Farris. "I'm bored to death. It's time for a road trip, and I know exactly where." He points at a post beneath the shock jock's comment, a photograph of the demonstrations at Lafayette Square.

"I don't think Debra would approve," says Tim. Debra's his wife. She had been Farris's high school sweetheart. Once he took Debra to the county fair in Luray. At some point, they stepped in the fortune-telling tent where a lady lined up three face cards. She said one of them, the queen of diamonds, is a haughty and jealous lady, but that he didn't need to worry because the other, the king of spades, was the ultimate card in spiritual energy and wisdom, a perfect match for the third, the queen of hearts.

She pointed at Debra. "You ought to marry her."

But as it turned out, he married Brenda, who was so jealous she threw fits when she caught him talking to other women, especially when they were out drinking at Uncle Buck's. One night, she stayed out late dancing with some dude to jukebox music, downing one tequila shot after another while he went home to their apartment a few blocks away. When she came in after three, he was asleep. She grabbed him by his ponytail, dragged him out of bed, and beat his head against the floor before he was sufficiently awake to stop her. That was it. Nobody messes with him. He moved back to the farm.

A few weeks later, he found Debra shopping at the Food Lion and told her what happened. They ended up in bed together. He felt a twinge of regret that lasted a day or two. He didn't know how she felt.

Whatever she felt, Debra allows Tim to tag along to DC. They race down the valley on their Indian Motorcycles up Route 66 toward the big city. Near Front Royal, Farris spies a sign for a Walmart. He pulls into the parking lot. At the glass entrance door, a security guard steps in front of them.

"You fellas can't go in there without masks," he stammers. He's a short guy with pipestem appendages that Farris could twist around his neck. But instead, he grabs a surgical mask from the table next to the runt. When they stroll outside after Farris purchased his engine oil and a Coke, he rips off his mask and spits on it.

"I'm in charge of my own life," he chortles, taking a sip of the Coke.

"I'm keeping my mask," counters Tim, tucking it in his back pocket, "in case we run into more trouble."

They do once they park their bikes behind a McDonald's on Seventeenth Street in Washington and stroll to a long line at the carryout. Farris bumps into a tall, lanky pirate wearing earrings, a red scarf over his head, and no mask.

"Hey, what's the idea," the pirate grouses. He coughs and

covers his mouth but not before some of the spray lands on Farris's arm. He wipes the spray off with his hand and rubs it against his jeans. Then he punches the pirate in the chest. He staggers backward, losing his balance, and bumps into a behemoth man in dreadlocks.

"Hey, what's the idea," growls the man through his mask as he backs off as if the pirate had cooties.

"You better wear a mask," says Tim.

"Aw, shut up," growls Farris. He's sick of his chickenshit buddy.

After they purchase their food, they saunter down the street to Lafayette Square and sit on a curb near a metal fence behind which are dozens of cops and soldiers in riot gear. They eat slowly and check out the signs attached to the fence.

The first one says "Mr. Trump Tear Down This Wall."

"What wall's he talking about?" asks Tim.

"What do you think, dummy? This one," says Farris as he stuffs some fries in his mouth.

"See that one." Tim points at a yellow sign with red letters.

Powerfully
Effective
Anointing
Crushing
Evil

"That's funny. PEACE," says Tim, raising his two fingers in a peace sign. They both laugh, stand up slowly, and toss their McDonald's trash in a barrel. They wander around DC, checking out the crowds, the DC cops, the Secret Service, the Park Police, and the graffiti, most of which says BLM this, BLM that, up Sixteenth to check out the "Black Lives Matter" painted in huge yellow letters on the street. They return to the fence where the crowd has grown thicker. They raise their arms in a power salute and chant, "Black Lives Matter, Black Lives Matter." Others in the crowd bend down on their knees with their hands raised, chanting, "Don't shoot. Don't shoot." And a few of the braver ones, Farris thinks, rattle the fence as if it is a cage they're trying to break through to charge the authorities on the other side. The authorities, whatever they are—some are dressed in fatigues—seem rattled themselves, slapping their batons and holding their shields up as if they expect projectiles, water bottles, and rocks to fly over the fence and strike them. Farris joins the fence rattlers. The rattlers are screaming, "Let us in! Let us in!" but they're not pushing that hard, so Farris gives an extra shove, and part of the fence collapses. The authorities rush up to seal the hole. The crowd backs off. Some run off up Sixteenth. He and Tim scatter in the direction of McDonald's, laughing their heads off.

They jump on their bikes and zoom out of town like they are being chased by a posse. They camp out at a park near the Potomac River. They build a fire, munch on dried beef and stale potato chips, and sip Kool-Aid spiked with bourbon.

"You know what you're lacking?" says Tim, shaking his head. He picks up a stick and stirs the fire.

"What am I lacking?" Farris frowns at his friend, wondering what stupid thing he will come up with now.

"You're lacking a girlfriend," Tim says. "I mean, if you had a girlfriend, it could be the four of us tooling down the highway rather than us two."

"I can find a girlfriend anytime I want to," he growls, and then, out of spite, he lights in with how he had a girlfriend when he shacked up with Debra after she married Tim.

"Yeah, I know," says Tim, stirring the fire. The embers pop. One lands on Farris's boot. He kicks it away. "She told me, and I forgave her because she said it was the last time. She was totally over you."

The next morning when Farris wakes up, Tim Newton's gone. He must've pulled the cycle down the road out of earshot before he started it. Farris kicks off his blanket, stands up, and stretches like he doesn't give a damn. He gathers his stuff together and puts it in the saddlebag.

A week after he arrives back at the farm, his mother awakes in the morning with a 103-degree temperature. They rush her to the hospital, and within another week she's dead. Sarah blames her brother.

"You don't wear a mask, which I guess would be all right if you didn't go all over the place, like to that rally in Washington. What do you care about black people? What do you care about anybody for that matter?"

Hank doesn't agree with his wife. You can catch the bug

anywhere. "I mean, it's like seedpods floating in the air, only you can't see it."

Farris strolls outside with his hands in his pockets, feeling like shit. He wanders across the field to the barn where Hank keeps his guns locked in a safe in one of the stalls. He knows the combination. Opens it. Finds the Walther PP handgun and the ammunition. He jumps on his Indian Motorcycle, guns the engine, and roars down the dirt driveway, past the willow trees on either side of the front gate. He pauses at the gate and checks back at the house where Sarah and Hank stand on the front steps, probably wondering what he's up to. Sarah either waves goodbye or motions for him to come back. It's hard to tell.

Farris roars down the road to where it ends at the base of Elk Mountain. He pushes the bike behind a tree and follows a trail uphill, then into the underbrush until he finds the creek. About a quarter mile down the bank, he comes to the cascades. He follows the trail to the pool. He sits down. Leans against a tree. Stares up at the ridge of Elk Mountain, expecting to see a hawk gliding in the thermals. But there's only blue sky and fluffy pink clouds. It's nearing sunset. A wind picks up. Rustles the tree leaves. He can almost hear a voice. It's spooky. He takes the Walther from his pocket and loads the magazine. He thinks about his mother and what he might have done to her. When he was a kid, his parents worked from dawn to dusk at the farm chores. In the evening before dinner, sometimes they'd drive in the pickup along the ridge to check the fences and, he thought, to be alone. He caught them kissing a couple of times. He laughs. He turns his head and looks at the Walther PP. Is he the cause of his mother's death? He sticks the gun barrel in his mouth just to get the feel of it. He puts his finger on the trigger, but out of the corner of his eye, he sees a bunny creep from behind a rock to stare at him. It must be the great-great grandchild of that bunny that stared at him twenty years ago. He points the gun at the bunny, but it doesn't stir, eyes intently on him as if awaiting its fate. Then he begins to think that the bunny is his mother and that the voice in the trees is his mother's voice. What is she saying? He remembers after the last time he was up here she said something about him riding the fences. He knows what that means and ponders it for a moment before he drops the gun. Tears run down his cheeks. He covers his face. He has never cried before. Even when he was little and his pop switched him with the willow stick, he didn't cry. It was a matter of pride.

Losing Lars

I AM IN LOVE WITH LARS'S MISTRESS. SO IS JACKSON. Underneath his bed is his father's telescope. We train it on her window. We hope to catch a glimpse of her in a state of undress, but that never happens. We caught Ms. Disbury in a red bra and black lace panties, Ms. Holmes in a towel as she stepped out of the shower, but never Inga Hoffmann.

Inga is Danish, German on her father's side. She is a statuesque, blond-haired lady with big, round china doll eyes and big hands that could probably squeeze the life out of us. But she has a smile that lights up her face. Once she told Jackson and me to think of her as our mother. A mother is someone you can trust. Someone to come to in times of need, she said. She speaks in a careful, clipped British accent, curling her tongue in her mouth so that the s's don't hiss out as z's as in "A mother isz szomeone...," but sometimes she can't help herself. She's so beautiful when she makes mistakes. She tosses her head so that her blond tresses spill over her shoulders as she whispers throatily, "Excuzz me." It's enough to make our hearts melt.

We know she won't last long. Already we notice the daggers that the Mss. Disbury and Holmes and the lesser masters' wives throw at her as she marches across the quad. She is single. She is exotic. The masters fight over sitting at her table in the dining hall. They open the door for her when her hands are full. Some of the more daring ones whisper in her ear or touch her shoulder quickly, as if her skin were made of hot lava. Even the headmaster, Peabody, once pinched her bottom, or so we heard. She threatened to quit.

"All I want is the zame respect you give to the other masters," she said.

In a certain way, Jackson and I share her problem. The first day we arrived at Betts Academy, we left campus without permission for the village of Betts at the bottom of the hill where, near the new gas station, we tipped over a San-O-John with a construction worker in it. A few months later the dorm master found us sucking on some oranges that had been injected with Jack Daniel's, a gift from Jackson's sister. Peabody wanted to expel us on the spot but instead gave us a month of Saturday detention. That meant we had to spend every Saturday morning from 7:00 a.m. to noon in the detention hall with a master who hated our guts for making him get up early on the weekend. I guess what I am saying is that like Inga Hoffmann, we won't last long, though for different reasons.

Jackson is from a close-knit family in Hagerstown about one hundred miles southeast of Betts. The reason he's incarcerated here is that he's ADHD. A psychiatrist told his parents that "the Academy," as we call it, specializes in

ADHD, which, I suppose, is true since there seems to be a lot of hyper kids around here. I'm not one of them. My issue is that I don't come from a close-knit family.

My dad works for the World Bank, so he's often in Europe or Asia. I used to live at home with mom. I'm an only child. Mom spent the first couple of months at home when I was a baby, then she returned to work for the Census Bureau and I was sent off to day care, then to a Montessori preschool, and finally an elementary school named after a Civil War general. I won't give the name of the general, but it's the same one who said, "War is hell." The same could be said of the school that was named after him. When Dad found Mom a job at the World Bank, they decided to travel together, and that meant I had to leave the elementary school to board at Betts.

This is how the difficulty begins. On winter break my second year at Betts, Inga asks me to take care of Lars while she visits friends in New York. Everyone else has gone, including Jackson, who's on his way to Florida to visit Disney World. My parents are in Paris. They send me a postcard with a picture of two lovers strolling across a bridge over the Seine on one side and a note on the other saying basically that they wished I was there. I throw the card in the trash.

I stroll across the quad with the key to Inga's apartment in one hand and my Latin and CS book in the other. I don't mind Latin, and for good reason—Inga teaches it—but I hate CS, which stands for central studies. Right now we are studying the attack on Pearl Harbor from the point of view of a Japanese American kid. The author seems to think it is un-American the way they incarcerated the kid and his family in an internment camp. I agree, but the story's boring. I want action, like the planes dive-bombing the battleships. My sympathy lies with the dead sailors floating in the water, not the kid. I guess that means I'm not PC. Okay, I'm not. For instance, I think my mom should be home taking care of me. I'd even take my dad. Or, as I stroll across the quad, I'm imagining Inga in a state of undress rather than what a nice person she is and how she trusts me to take care of her little, fluffy-haired bichon, Lars.

I climb the stairs to the third floor of the faculty apartments and open the door. Lars shoots out between my legs in a white blur. He skids down the hallway, his toenails clicking on the bare wood floor. I follow him to the first floor and let him out, which is a mistake, but I've seen him wandering around campus countless times, and besides, Inga said it was okay. Lars is an outside dog, and she would rather lose him than deny him his natural instincts. Prophetic words, as it turns out. I watch Lars streak across the quad and down the hill to Peabody's house, where his buddy Roger lives. I head back up to Inga's apartment. I should say "Ms. Hoffmann" because that's what we are supposed to call her, but after Jackson and I rescued her from Peabody, who was on a butt-pinching mission, I guess, she said we could call her by her first name. That was one of the few times we were in her apartment, and all we saw was her living room—a couple of chairs around a card table; an easy chair in a corner with a side table and reading lamp; a couch and TV; Lars, who was exploring the contents of a trash can he tipped over; and some pictures on the wall. The only one I noticed was a print of a Chinese scholar in long silk robes surrounded by a semicircle of his students who looked raptly at him as though he was imparting to them the wisdom of the ages.

This time I pass through the living room, glancing perfunctorily at the picture and the tipped-over trash can, its contents trailing to the easy chair where I haphazardly throw my books. I open the door to her bedroom and peer in. It's dark except for the pale winter light that seeps through the window. I close the shades and switch on the overhead lamp. In the far corner is a four-poster bed behind which hangs a black-and-white photograph of a waterfall in a lonely country glen. In another corner is a bureau, and under the window a writing desk and chair. Spartan surroundings, I think, almost a nun's room. It gives me the shivers. I wander into the bathroom. That too seems Spartan: black-and-white checkerboard tile on the floor and a white porcelain tub and sink that's cracked and turning milky gray. I turn on the spigot in the bathtub, and the water spits out in fits and starts. The trash can is tipped over in the bathroom. I can see Lars's teeth marks all over a discarded bottle of Gold Bond body lotion and a Dr. Scholl's moleskin box. Does Inga Hoffmann have corns? I wonder. I open her medicine cabinet and notice all the various feminine products down to the Firminol-10 Tummy Firming Formula. I do not know much about the opposite sex and regard all these jars, boxes, and plastic containers full of oils, ointments, and such as artifacts left from a forgotten age. She might as well be a Viking princess. She told me that I was welcome in her apartment to study and watch television while she was gone, but I feel uneasy with the thoughts that are running through my head like freight trains.

I creep back into the bedroom to the bureau and open the top drawer. My mouth is watering like Pavlov's dog, or more like Lars. I reach in and grab a pair of her white silk underwear, hold it up waist-high, and imagine how it would fill out if it contained her body. I run my thumb and forefinger through the soft material and place it back carefully so that she can't tell that I disturbed it. I lift up her bra. It dangles in my hand like a wounded animal. I check the size. 38C. I make a fist and place it inside one of the cups, more than enough room. I touch the soft cotton inner lining of the cup and imagine her breasts resting against this soft lining and then my hands cupping her breasts. I drop the bra and rifle through the rest of the drawers.

One night, when I still lived with my parents, a vandal invaded the bedroom of the teenage girl next door when the family was off on vacation. He scattered her underwear all over the floor and wrote obscene comments with her own lipstick on the mirror over her bureau. The police interviewed me later and all the other boys in the neighborhood.

I was outraged at the time that the police would consider me a suspect, but now I understand perfectly.

I creep back to the living room, collapse on the couch, and stare at the print of the scholar and the students. Outside it has begun to snow. The flakes are fat and wet. They stick to the window briefly before slowly sliding down to the sill, leaving a patchwork of thin, watery trails behind them. I wonder what has become of Lars when I hear a pack of dogs barking below me and rush to the window. I see him almost immediately streaking out in front of the others across the quad and into the woods after the fox. It is not a hunt. The fox is in heat. The local dogs catch a whiff of the fox, and they go berserk. Roger, who is a heavy, slow-moving wire-haired Lab, is the last in the woods. I watch him disappear and know it will be days before I see these dogs again.

The last time this happened in the fall, the dogs returned one by one, worn out and dejected except for one, a Jack Russell who was never found. The owner of the Jack Russell, one of the lesser masters, Berwyn, accused Lars of putting the other dogs up to chasing the fox. Lars had a reputation as a dog with a large appetite. He was known to have knocked up a local basset hound, to sneak in the kitchen to have a bite to eat, or to climb up the hill that overlooked the dumpster in back of the dining hall and jump in. He tipped over the trash cans on campus, stole the masters' gloves or whatever was lying around in their offices, and even sneaked into their private rooms to deposit a gift in the foyer. It is no wonder that Berwyn blamed Lars just as Lars's mistress is blamed for the agitation the masters and the boys at Betts Academy have felt since her arrival.

I stand at the window with my hands in my pockets and stare at the snow. It is so thick that I can't see the mountains behind my dorm. I can barely see the dorm and the light that comes from my room and shines brightly on the wet sidewalk that leads up to the door. A wind picks up and rattles the window. I decide to forgo a search for Lars and his buddies until tomorrow morning. I wander over to the kitchenette and open the freezer door where Inga, as she promised, stored half a dozen frozen cheese pizzas for my use. Pizza is in my blood. It seemed that every evening when I lived with Mom, I'd order pizza and a two-liter bottle of Coke, and chicken poppers or cheese bread from Domino's. I should be fat, but I guess I'm hyper like the rest of the boys here.

I stick the pizza in the oven and wait for it to heat up. I know the boys are in love with Lars's mistress like Jackson and I are, only in a different way. Last year in Latin II, after her second month on campus, Inga assigned a test on irregular verbs. I remember that she was standing with her back to us as I wandered into the classroom. She had one hand on her desk while she stared at the top right-hand corner of the blackboard where it appeared that Berwyn, the algebra master, had written "DO NOT ERASE: Algebra Homework." Underneath this were what appeared to be equations, such as "(ere + 1) − 2ui = us" and "are − avi = (1 + 3) / atus." Inga stared for a long time at these equations in disbelief, no doubt, because, if you took out the pluses, minuses, and such, the letters you were left with were the same as the Latin endings in our test. She turned around and stared at us as if we were a roomful of strangers.

"Class dismissed," she said, waving her hand and backing into the arms of a jock named Halsey, who snickered at her as she fled the classroom. Chu, the wise guy who sat one seat over, poked me in the side and snickered. So did McKelvey and Davis, who I imagined designed the algebra homework. They were pretty boys on the lacrosse team whose advances Inga spurned.

I would've liked to pummel them to death with their lacrosse sticks if I hadn't seen Jackson running out of the room after Inga. I followed him across the quad and up the stairs of the faculty apartments. We knocked on Inga's door and she let us in.

We told her how sorry we were that this happened, and she said it didn't matter. "Itz my fault," she said.

There we were, sitting on the couch, not looking at each other, but at the print of the Chinese scholar in long silk robes surrounded by a semicircle of his students, just as I am staring at it now while chewing on the doughy pizza. And I have to admit, I was amazed. I have probably had twenty teachers in my life, and this is the first one ever to take the blame for anything. It was always my fault or the fault of some other student, even though we were only kids and we were in the process of learning how to act. The teachers already knew, or why else would they be teachers? I don't want to go too far with this because everybody makes mistakes. But it amazed me that Inga Hoffmann admitted to it even though I don't believe it was her mistake. Just the admission is amazing, and it was the first time that I began to respect her as a real teacher. I'll go one step further: a real grown-up. So as I sit here chewing on the pizza, I feel somewhat ashamed of myself, who, on the one hand, really cares for a person and, on the other, rifles through her drawers in search of her intimate apparel and daydreams about what this person would look like naked. But then I think of Lars.

In the morning, I am rudely awakened by a banging on the door and realize that I have fallen asleep on Inga's couch. My clothes are wrinkled, and I'm all sweaty.

"Open up. I know you're in there, Olsen." It's Peabody, who is normally a calm, relaxed individual but is now extremely agitated, I think because I slept in Inga's apartment rather than my dorm room. I manufacture a story about how she gave me permission. But it isn't about that at all. It's about precious Roger, who he last saw playing with that "miscreant" Lars. I tell him that I saw them go in the woods, and he demands that I find Roger. Lars could go to hell as far as he is concerned.

The one thing I love about Betts Academy is the location in a valley surrounded on three sides by mountains like a horseshoe. The open end of the horseshoe points north. Lake-effect snow blasts down the valley and stalls. There is snow on the ground four months of the year, though now that it is late February, it is beginning to taper off. I make my way across the quad to the ski shop attached to Halsey Gym, named after the grandfather of the Halsey whom Inga backed into in her classroom. I pick out a pair of cross-country skis and head out to the trail that cuts through the woods where the dogs disappeared. I know exactly where I am going because last fall it was me who discovered the fox's den, and I didn't reveal it to anyone.

I know what happened to those stupid dogs. They chased the fox back to her den. She spent the night relaxing, all curled up with her bushy tail keeping her warm—by now she is used to the chase—while the dogs loitered around the entrance, sniffing the air. Some of them wandered home, though most stayed, hanging their heads dejectedly, hoping against hope that they would have a chance. They reminded me of the masters and the boys at Betts.

I break out into a meadow at the other end of the woods. The bottoms of my skis are heavy with the snow, so it is hard going. I skirt the creek that meanders through the meadow and cross the bridge into a new set of woods that start at the base of Betts Mountain. I find the den at the bottom of a cliff near a frozen pond. The dogs are not around, so I move off—downwind, I hope—to a place where I can see the den and not be seen. I make a little fire with the brush and twigs around me, pull a snack out of my rucksack, and wait.

The amazing thing about Inga Hoffmann is that, unlike most teachers I have met, she learned from experience. She knew she was teaching a class full of dull-witted teenage boys who thrived on stimulation. She ended all written tests for the time being after the incident with the algebra homework. She taught our class all the Latin words, the phrases, and conjugations. She drilled us on them but out loud. We wrote a one-act play in Latin and acted it out in class over and over again. We translated Mark Antony's speech at Caesar's funeral into Latin, and each of us memorized a part. We read Juvenal, Virgil, and excerpts from Caesar's *Commentaries*. She wheeled a television into our room, and we watched *Spartacus* and *Ben-Hur*. Latin is a dead language, but Inga made it alive, at least for me and Jackson and some others as far as I could tell. The classroom turned so noisy that Peabody looked in and asked what was the matter. Inga smiled at him, and he forgot himself, tripping over a chair as he left the room.

I put a few more twigs on the fire and place my hands above the flames to keep warm. The dogs are baying in the distance, though they seem to be moving farther away. Then suddenly I see Lars. He peeks out from behind a tree. His tongue is hanging out. He is staring across a field of tall grass that's sticking out of the snow. The grass starts to move, and I see a brown blur. Before I can clamber to my feet to tackle Lars, he streaks off after the blur. All I can see are two sets of grass moving, the one closest to me gaining on the one farther away.

The dogs are baying. They are so off the scent that it makes me laugh. I sit down and wait. I think of the poor, hassled female fox. What do they call a female fox? Not "bitch." But I'm thinking, if those dogs out there who are loping along and hanging their heads dejectedly are the boys and masters at Betts, then I am like Lars. I want to be Lars.

But so does Chu. I've seen him up there in her apartment. I've seen Halsey and the pretty boys, one of them smirking out her window. Once I saw McKelvey grab her by the shoulder as we left the classroom and whisper into her ear. She snapped her head around and pushed him away.

"You are not a gentleman," she said.

The dogs are still baying in the distance, but they're moving closer, at least one dog, who lets out with a deep-throated, plaintive "woof, woof" that I recognize. Roger staggers out into the clearing. He rocks from side to side. I stand up, put snow over the fire to make sure it's out, and retrieve Peabody's dog.

In the days that follow, the other dogs stagger back to school one by one. I put dog food outside the faculty apartments, but Lars does not appear. I wait for him at the dumpster behind the dining hall, but he's a no-show. I return to the fox's den and practically freeze to death one night waiting until after dark. The fox does not return. Nor does Lars. I walk downhill to the village of Betts. It is actually a crossroads that consists of a church, a white clapboard building with a steeple; a general store; a gas station; and a blue trailer that is the post office. In front of the trailer, I see Lars peeing on the tire of a car. I give chase. I follow him past the gas station and behind the general store, where I climb down a culvert that leads to the stream that is frozen over. Lars heads downstream, and I follow him, carefully stepping from rock to rock under the bridge until, on the other side, I break through the ice and I'm up to my ankles in icy water. I nearly fall on my butt. I see Lars climb up the embankment, and then he is gone.

I am in love with Lars's mistress. But I don't know how to tell her. Jackson is back, and he comes with me to her apartment. We have gone on about a dozen other searches, and it seems like there is no hope.

"Itz all right, boyz," she says.

We stand there for a long time, and she smiles. The smile lights up her face, but I can tell that I have done something to her. I don't know what it is. It's not like McKelvey or Peabody. I have gone through her drawers, seen her intimate things, and I have thought about her in ways that they have thought about her, though I keep it all a secret. She doesn't know how I feel. But she knows I lost Lars.

This is how the difficulty ends. The snow is falling all over the valley. It is falling on the blue metal roof of the post office, on the roof that covers the gas pump where Peabody pumps gas while the missus is passing gas inside the gas station bathroom, on the roof of the faculty apartments where Berwyn is jacking off and Mr. and Ms. Disbury are coupling—it takes five minutes. They lie back and smoke cigarettes. I think of sex and all its ramifications. I think of Lars lying in a field, his eyes glassy and wide open, his teeth bared in one last gasp as he is slowly covered with snow.

And the vixen in her den relaxing, all curled up with her bushy tail keeping her warm. Is there something cooking in her oven?

The snow is falling all over the valley, and then it stops. A wind picks up. The clouds dissipate, and the stars scatter out from the northern horizon to the peaks of the mountains that envelop us. Jackson is combing the faculty apartments with his telescope, and he tells me to come over.

"See," he says.

I put my eye to the lens, and I see Inga Hoffmann standing at the window of her apartment, combing her hair, naked and as white as the snow. I gasp. I feel that I have died and gone to Valhalla.

Rage! Blow!

I LOVE BETTS ACADEMY IN THE FALL, ESPECIALLY UP HERE ON the football field, in my football regalia, overlooking the campus and the whole valley stretched out below me. I can see the boys in their blue blazers and khakis scurrying back and forth on the front quad. Scurrying in and out of the redbrick classroom buildings and dorms. Or the redbrick administration building, the chapel, and library lined up in front of me like Monopoly hotels on Broadway. Everything in perfect order, the lawns mowed, the flowering shrubs flowering, the maple and oak trees fully freighted. Then the wind blows in from the north, and this is what I love. The chaos.

The leaves on the maples and oaks turn colors. They fall. They scurry across the quad, blown in every direction by the wind. The boys wear coats over their blazers and bend their heads to the wind. Bare spots appear on the lawn where the landscapers are fertilizing for the winter. They cut back the shrubs. The blue sky turns shades of gray. The winds blow the clouds across the sky from one end of the valley to the other. The heaviest and darkest clouds come to rest above our heads against Betts Mountain. I love it when the weather turns violent and chaotic because it reminds me of what goes on inside of me. It's like a Shakespearean play.

The other day in English class, the wind was blowing. It was rattling the windows in the chapel. The chapel doubles as the theater, and this is where we are taught Shakespeare by our headmaster, Peabody—his only class. Peabody is old, at least seventy. His hair is white, always disheveled, as it was in particular on this day when the wind was blowing so wildly. He stood on the stage in the chapel, raised his fist, and shook it at the ceiling.

"Blow," he said in a loud voice above the rattle of the windows. "Blow, winds, and crack your cheeks! Rage! Blow!"

We all cheered, and a few of us in the audience yelled, "King Lear, King Lear," because that was what he wanted us to do—guess what play the lines came from. But this time I particularly related to him standing up there on the stage, shaking his fist at the ceiling. I know, since we studied it, that at this point in the play, Lear has found out that his daughters betrayed him. He is mad beyond belief. I can relate to that. One day the world is perfect. The next a wind blows in from the north. I love it.

I remember driving out here with my dad years ago and staying at Peabody's house down the hill below the library. It was around Christmas. The students were gone. Mrs. Peabody fixed me hot chocolate. She sat me on the couch next to the fire. My legs didn't reach the floor. Next to me was Roger, Peabody's arthritic wire-haired Lab, but he was a pup then. He was licking my face and trying to steal sips from my hot chocolate. I lifted the cup in the air so he couldn't reach it, and I saw my dad leaning his arm against the mantelpiece and looking down at me as though I were the center of his universe. He was laughing. This was perfect.

In those days, when I was a kid, I wanted my dad to be proud of me more than anything else in the world. Then I went to school, and it dawned on me that this might not happen. In third grade, they sent me to a psychologist for writing on my arm with a ballpoint pen. I was drawing barbed wire around my wrist that I'd seen on a rap singer on MTV and an eye on the palm of my hand. Then the learning specialist at the school found me in the hallway outside my classroom banging my fists against the wall. She asked me what was the matter, and I told her that Brenda Bottomly called me an "asshole loser." She said I shouldn't use that word, and I asked her which one. She said, "The first one."

Then she asked me if I was upset by the second word.

That, I thought, was a stupid question, and I should have given it the answer it deserved but instead said that I wasn't a loser. She wondered why I fixated on the word *loser*, and I could go on from there, but the upshot was that she called my parents and said I was a troubled child and needed to go to a psychologist again. My dad disagreed, and the specialist said, "If your child had a broken leg, you'd take him to a doctor, wouldn't you?" My dad was pissed.

"I'm not an idiot," he said. But Mom prevailed.

"We know you're not an idiot," she said, "but you're not an expert either."

That was when they put me on Ritalin and later, when I stopped doing my homework, Zoloft. I started feeling like the bouncing head they have in the Zoloft commercial on TV. This was not perfect.

I'M STANDING ON the field in full football regalia, my helmet tucked under my arm, my hair blowing behind me in the wind. I have long dirty-blond tresses and a dirty-blond goatee that makes me look older and meaner than I am. The freckles across my nose ruin the effect. I have a cut under my eye I received when I ran into the linebacker with such force that he fell backward and I fell on top of him. I elbowed him in the throat. I called him a bastard. He called me a shit and grabbed my face mask. I think his fingernails are what cut me.

The blood from the cut is seeping down my cheek like a red tear. I wipe it away and rub it across the numbers on my jersey. The trainer comes over and dabs the cut with hydrogen peroxide. He tapes on a Band-Aid, makes me sit on the bench, and hunches down beside me. "How do you feel?" He's looking me in the eye.

"Great. Great. Wonderful," I say.

"What happened? Did you get hit hard in the head?"

"No, it was nothing," I say. I know he wants to see if I have a concussion. "I can't wait to go back in."

The trainer slaps me on the shoulder pad. Coach Bray looks over, concerned, and I give him the thumbs-up. We are playing the Penfield Red Devils, the team that always beats us. Last year it was 17–3, one of our better efforts, but I didn't play because I had a dislocated shoulder. Coach called me a sissy.

I know that he's disappointed in me. So is Peabody. At Dad's funeral, Peabody asked Mom if there was anything he could do, and she said that she could take care of my sisters but she could not take care of me. My behavior was erratic. I don't want to say this, but the truth is I think I hate my mom. I don't think she caused Dad's death. He died when I was thirteen, slowly, of cancer. But I don't think she exactly made his life easy. They argued a lot, and most of their arguments were about me. It was the Zoloft and the Ritalin. Mom said that I was temperamental and impulsive.

"Preston"—that's my name—"is like a firecracker, and all you have to do is light the fuse," my mom told our psychiatrist, "and he explodes—boom."

Dad said that I never exploded before I went to school. I was off on my own, independent, a very happy little boy.

"Why do you always blame someone else? We know where the problem lies."

I hate my mother. Maybe I don't hate her, but I don't understand her.

I'm up here on the bench watching Penfield march down the field, but they don't march far enough. They try a field goal. The ball glances off the uprights. I look up at the sky. The wind is picking up. The fall leaves scurry across the football field. The clouds move across the sky from one end of the valley to the other. The heaviest and darkest clouds come to rest above our heads, against Betts Mountain. I hear the crowd behind me stamping their feet on the bleachers. It's our ball. I rush out to the field.

I know why Peabody and Bray are disappointed. They thought I'd be like Dad. They thought I'd be a natural. When Dad was here, Betts never lost to Penfield or to many other teams. When he died, Mom gave all his trophies to the school. They are now on display in a glass case in the entrance hall of Halsey Gym next to the bust of my grandfather. I have a lot of history to live down, and so far I'm not doing as well as my father did, though there is the hope that I will be filthy rich like Grandpa and they'll name a building after me. For now though, as I squat over the ball—I'm the center—it doesn't matter, because even though I'm not a natural, I feel like I'm in my natural element.

We clap when we break the huddle and peel off in a line in order of battle. Lese hunches over me. He calls the signals. I slap the ball in his hands so the laces touch his fingertips. He fades back. We hold the defensive line in check, then let them pour through toward Lese, who's backpedaling. Higgins, the end, glides laterally across the field behind us. Lese lets go of a perfect spiral into his hands. We lunge forward, picking out our assignments. Mine is the linebacker, who outweighs me by at least thirty pounds, but he's off-balance. I plow into him and push him sideways, opening a hole big enough for Higgins to sneak through before a defensive lineman plows into both of us. The collision jars my brain. I stagger backward. The two defensive players fall on top of me. One of them elbows me in the chest. I punch him in the stomach. My fist disappears in his flesh. He lets out a sigh. I smell his rotten breath.

"Get off me, you bastard."

He does meekly, but his friend, the lineman, calls me a fucker.

I call him a pig, and he punches me in the helmet. I see fireworks in front of my eyes. I want to kill him, but a referee is hovering nearby.

The next play, Kolker, our fullback, slants through my hole as I catch the linebacker about waist-high and bend him in half. I cut my arm on the clasp that holds his pants up. He limps off the field. Penfield calls time. I suck my wound and rub the blood on the numbers of my jersey. I feel great. I feel amazing. We have advanced thirty-five yards from our own eleven in two plays, and all through my hole.

It is midway through the first quarter, and there is no score, an amazing feat considering last year's loss and the string of others back to the time when my father was a student. In his senior year, Betts Academy beat Penfield 20–14 on a sixty-yard run he made in the waning moments of the game.

I look to the sidelines, and there's Bray covering his mouth with a clipboard, whispering to Lese, who's nodding his head. Peabody is up in the stands shaking his fists like a madman, as are my classmates and the parents screaming, "Go Bruins! Go Bruins!" It's homecoming, and the parents have come from as far as Miami—that's Kolker's parents—though most of them are from nearby Pittsburgh,

Scranton, and Philadelphia. I wish Dad was here. Even Mom. She's in California with her new husband, Chet, and Wendy and Kristine. They're like the Brady Bunch, except my sisters are the brunettes—I'm the aberration in the family—and the boys, Chet's sons, are redheads.

I'm sad that they're not here to watch me, but it's their loss, not mine. I've grown since my days on Zoloft and Ritalin. Now I'm high on a more powerful drug, and that's what I mean when I say I may not be a natural, but I feel like I'm in my natural element.

At least, I feel that way until the whistle blows, and I look up from the ball and see the lineman lined up opposite me.

"Hey, fucker, how you doing?" he growls, barely loud enough for me to hear. "I murder you."

The lineman is licking his lips. His eyes are shiny black buttons, full of hate, I think, or maybe hunger. He must outweigh me by a hundred pounds, and he can't speak in complete sentences.

I hike the ball, and he runs over me. He tackles Kolker in the backfield. The next play I upend the bruiser with a cross-body block, but on his way down, he grabs Lese by the numbers and drags him down on top of us. Lese knees me in the crotch. Luckily I'm wearing a plastic jock, though the plastic edge bruises my thighbone. I limp back to the huddle. The final play is a pass, which is intercepted when the behemoth tips the ball from the line of scrimmage where I thought I was effectively blocking him. Bray glares at me as

I limp off the field. The crowd in the stands is silent. I can hear the wind blowing through the rafters.

I throw my helmet to the ground. Kolker slaps his hands on my shoulder pads and tells me not to worry. "We'll get them next time."

Lese and Higgins agree, and even Bray comes up to give me a pep talk about how those thirty-five yards were made through my hole and it would have been more yards, except they threw in "a monkey wrench." It's his fault for not adjusting to the situation.

"Football's a game of adjustments," he says, "like real life."

Penfield kicks a field goal and the quarter is over, and that's when I find out what Coach Bray means by adjustments. He runs Kolker through everybody's hole except my own, and when Kolker only makes short gains, he tries passes, but the Penfield secondary swarms on the receivers and there's an interception that leads to another field goal.

In the locker room at halftime, Bray tells us how amazed he is by our performance. The Red Devils came into this game 7–0. They haven't lost a game in three years, and last week they beat Mercersburg 48–10. "And you're keeping them within six points, one touchdown and an extra point. We could beat them."

I'm on the periphery of the crowd, sitting on the benches in front of the lockers. I'm trying to look inconspicuous, ducking my head behind Kolker, but Bray's looking straight at me. When Dad was here, Bray was an assistant. He followed Dad to Pennsylvania and was there at the Colgate game when Dad broke his ankle. I don't know how he felt, but I don't imagine it was that much different than when I dislocated my shoulder last year against Hill. I came off the field hunched over like Quasimodo, and there was a look on Bray's face exactly like my mom's look when she received a call from one of the teachers saying that I had not done my homework. She knew that I was capable of great things. She told me a hundred times that I tested well. I had a high IQ. That I was in the ninety-ninth percentile in memory and cognition in the entrance exam they gave us for kindergarten. I knew how to read before the other kids. I was a whiz at math and science, though she couldn't understand why I didn't like to read or write. She did. So did Kristine and Wendy.

"What is the matter with you?" she asked me. "Why don't you use your God-given talents?"

And this is what I see in Bray's eyes, though it's not using my talent that bothers him. I don't have any, unlike my father. I think he realizes that. With him, I think it's a déjà vu disgust. Like father, like son. It's hard for me to take. So I duck my head and sneak out to the field before anyone else.

I'm standing on the field in full regalia, my helmet tucked under my arm, my long blond tresses blowing in the wind. I'm stroking my goatee and trying to feel mean. The leaves on the maples and oaks on Betts Mountain are turning brilliant reds and oranges. In the higher elevations, the bare limbs stick out against the gray sky. They rock back and forth in the wind. The wind whistles through a stand of hemlock at the base of the mountain, a few yards beyond the field. A cold, light rain begins to fall. It pings against my helmet and shoulder pads. I lift my head up and feel the rain sting my face. I feel this knot inside me like I haven't eaten in days. My stomach seems shriveled up to the size of a pea. I want to murder someone. I hold this thought inside me. I want to murder someone. I want to tear them apart limb by limb and scatter their body parts all over the field. I want to do this preferably to the pig in the football helmet with the shiny button eyes that humiliated me.

But button eyes is gone, replaced by the gimpy linebacker who is only thirty pounds heavier than I. I hike the ball and lunge at him. Our eyes meet for a brief second. I think he sees that I plan to impale him with my helmet, so he tiptoes to the side like a prima ballerina. A big hole opens on my right through which you could drive a truck, though the play is off-tackle and stopped at the line of scrimmage. Bray notices the hole. He calls in a fifty-two right. I hike the ball. Lese turns and hands off to Kolker. I can feel Kolker's hand on my back as he follows my block. I cannot find the gimpy linebacker, who is probably by now doing pliés, but out of the corner of my eye, I can see the piggish lineman lumber toward us with his shiny button eyes fixed on a point ahead of us. Kolker moves to my right so I am between him and the lineman. I throw my body forward and catch the bruiser below the knees. When he falls forward, he's grasping air.

I land on my right shoulder and feel a sharp pain

followed by numbness like my whole arm has gone asleep. I ignore this and jump to my feet in time to see Kolker tackled thirty yards down the field by the safety.

"I'm gonna kill you next time," snarls the lineman as he trots by me on his dainty hooves. I can see a glimmer of doubt in his eyes. "You bet, gonna kill you."

The next play, he's lined up over me. My arm hurts like hell, so I tuck it up close to my body and reach out with my left hand to hike the ball. Coach Bray calls time-out. He sends in the backup center, Chu, who is a wise guy and as skittish as the linebacker. I amble over to the sidelines.

"You're hurt," Coach says.

"No, I'm not hurt. Send me back in," I demand. I glare at Coach, but he shakes his head as though he doesn't believe me and puts on his headset.

The rain has stopped. The wind is blowing the fall leaves across the field. There is a chill in the air that takes the edge off my pain. We are on the fifty-yard line and march backward to the forty-five on the next two plays, but my mind is on my father and how I wish he could see this, how more than anything else in the world I wish that he was simply alive. I don't care if he was proud of me. I don't care if he thought I was like a firecracker or that my behavior was erratic, that I was a failure because I couldn't live up to the things I was capable of. I care only that he could be here in the flesh, plain and simple.

Coach Bray sends me in on the third down. It's a pass. The lineman rises up like a serpent out of the sea, but before he can tip the ball, I spike him in the crotch with my helmet. He collapses to the ground and spins around like Curly in the Three Stooges. He whimpers. It doesn't matter that Higgins sees the cornerback bearing down on him and drops the ball. I trot off the field.

The Red Devils manage a couple of first downs and kick. We're on our own seventeen. I trot on the field. Coach Bray sees blood. He calls three 52 rights in a row, and I plow up button eyes like he's a field full of potting soil. We're on the thirty-seven. Higgins takes a pass over center, breaks a tackle, and plunges over into their territory. I can hear the crowd screaming in the stands, "Go Bruins! Go Bruins!" I can see Peabody banging his rolled-up program on the back of the bench. He has come down from the stands. Roger is hunched next to him, barking.

The next play Lese is blindsided as he manages a shovel pass to Kolker. Kolker is on my tail. The only thing between him and daylight are four defenders lined up like stars in perfect conjunction that portends a momentous event such as the slaying of Goliath by David. Not that I'm David. I happen to be in the right place at the right time. I step in the path of the defenders, and three of them topple over my supine body. The fourth spins around, regains his footing, but can't catch up to Kolker until the two-yard line. I hear everyone yelling at the top of their lungs, stamping their feet so the stands vibrate.

We march in for a touchdown through my hole, and we make an extra point.

Later in the game, button eyes—aka the bruiser, the pig, the sea serpent, Goliath, Curly—blindsides me, and I go skittering across the ground with my arms outstretched. I dislocate my shoulder for the second time in a year, but by that time we're ahead 13-6. Everyone in the stands seems to gasp, but as soon as I stand up, my shoulder pops back in the socket.

As THE LAST seconds tick off, I am standing behind the bench, my arm in a sling, the wind blowing like a tornado, picking up everything that isn't nailed down: leaves, football programs, paper cups, paper hot dog trays. Roger is still barking, and Mr. Peabody is still yelling at the top of his lungs, "Go Bruins! Go Bruins!" Then, with the student body and parents in the stands, he sings the fight song: "We are the Bruins, the mighty, mighty Bruins."

Mr. Peabody turns to me, a lopsided grin on his face, and yells above the din, "Outstanding game, Halsey." His hair is disheveled. He is still King Lear. He is very happy. I can relate to that.

Fine Art

Fast Food

THE WIND IS BLOWING IN THE DRIVER'S-SIDE WINDOW. IT scatters the thin tendrils of Jodi's brown hair. Her lips are covered in a shiny neutral gloss that makes them seem wet. Jodi is in profile. I see only one blue eye. It stares straight ahead down the highway. I think she is pensive, like she is wondering what will happen next.

Beyond her profile and blowing-up hair, three men sit at a picnic table. The one facing me has his hand raised as though he's making a point. He is shirtless. He has long hair and a mustache; the look in his eye is sinister, as though he is making plans with the others to rob a gas station. The other two on either side of him seem innocent enough. The one with a ponytail and baseball cap wears shorts and a white T-shirt. The other is pudgy, a white-haired older man in gray work clothes. They both stare at the shirtless man so I can't see their eyes.

Behind them is a fast-food stand. The sign above the stand is red. It is hard to read because of the dirt on the car window. The top line says "Take ove C v." The next line I can see perfectly—"FOOD PLATTERS"—and below, "Hoagies

Sandwiches Pierogies Chicken." I'm new to this area, so I don't know what a pierogi is. I ask Jodi.

"A pierogi is deep-fried bread," she says. "You fill it with potato, cheese, or cabbage. Sometimes even sauerkraut."

"Sounds nasty."

"No, it's really good," she says. "It's Polish food."

"Are you Polish?" I ask her.

"No." She stares straight ahead. The light changes. I take one last look at the stand and what's around it. The window where you take the orders is black. I can't see anyone inside. To the left is the gas station the men plan to rob. The building is white. The gas pumps are red. A sedan parked near the pumps is blue. A gray van pulls up. The sky is blue scattered with puffy white clouds. Behind me through the rearview, I can see the white line in the middle of the gray highway. There is a car in the far, far distance that appears like a white smudge.

I take this all in with my eyes like it's a realist painting, a Hopper, hanging in my brain. I wonder what would it be like twenty years from now if I marry this woman, would I still remember the picture. I reach over and touch her hand.

"Would you like to come to my apartment?" I ask her.

"Sure, I guess so," says Jodi. "But no funny business."

A Woman in the Sun

I eat a potato-filled pierogi. They are really good, as Jodi told me. We are sitting at the picnic table where last year the shirtless man and his two friends sat planning a robbery. Only, as it turns out, it wasn't the gas station next door they were going to rob. It was me.

Jodi's hand is on my knee. I lean close to her, the smell of potato on my breath.

It took six months before I could tell her about myself. I grew up in an apartment above a barbershop that my father owned. One day I drifted into the shop to say goodbye before I headed off to school. Dad was standing in front of the display window staring pensively at a mobile he hung there years ago when he opened the shop. The mobile consisted of eight miniature barber poles, each hanging from a string. When a customer opened the door to the shop, the draft would blow the mobile around and around so you would see a circle of light on the ceiling. First red. Then blue. Then silver. But there had been a storm the night before. My dad had left the window open. The wind blew in the rain and intertwined the string of the mobile so that the barber poles hung together in one jumbled mess.

My father cleaned up the water on the floor. He took down the mobile. He sat in the barber chair and started to untangle the strings.

I wanted to help.

"You go to school," he told me. "I'll see you tonight."

That day I had band practice, and I didn't get home until five. My dad was still in the barber chair, the mobile in his lap. It didn't seem like he had made much progress.

"Have you been doing this all day?"

"Between customers," he said, smiling up at me as I leaned on the barber chair.

The next day when I came home after school, he was still there untangling the mobile.

"Gee, Dad," I said.

"I'm making progress."

This went on for most of the week, until Thursday night. I pushed open the door, and there was the mobile hanging from the ceiling. It turned around and around so you would see a circle of light on the ceiling. The red. The blue. The silver.

"Isn't it beautiful?" my father asked me.

"Yes," I said. "It is."

"What are you trying to tell me?" Jodi asked. We were in the bedroom of my apartment. I had hardly laid a hand on her the whole six months I had known her, though I had tried to see her every day. Sometimes I would say hello and leave it at that. Other times I would ask her out on dates, to the movies, to a club to listen to music. I found out she loved independent movies and the blues. I took her to *Bottle Rocket*. We sat at a corner café after the movie, talking about the meaning of life and sacrifice. After we attended a Smokin' Joe Kubek concert, she kissed me. She was wearing that neutral gloss that made her lips seem wet. It tasted like strawberry. I gave her a couple of Stevie Ray Vaughan CDs for her birthday, and she kissed me again. I hardly ever initiated anything. Maybe I'd hold her hand. Or put my arm around her shoulder in the dark in the movie theater. Not that I was doing this all intentionally. I was twenty-five. I'd been out with a woman maybe five or six times.

I told her that before my father died, he asked me to take care of Mom. And that was why I stayed home even though I hated it. I hated the block we lived in, the long row of redbrick storefronts and empty apartments on the second floor with yawning, dark windows. I hated the cars that rushed up and down the street, blaring horns even late at night so I couldn't sleep. I hated the kids I went to school with who lived far off in a nicer part of town. I didn't hate my parents. My mother was the most beautiful girl in the town she came from in Norway. I've seen pictures of her when she was young. She looked like one of the actresses in a Bergman film. After my father died, I watched her age quickly. All the beauty was gone, almost overnight. She developed arthritis. Her mind went. She talked all the time about when she and Dad were young. She lasted two years, but she wasn't the mother I knew when my father was alive.

"They must've loved each other," I told Jodi.

"Yes, they must've," she said.

"I want a woman to love me the same way my mom loved my dad. I will love her back in the same way."

I ordered carryout and wandered down the street to pick it up. When I returned, I took the food to the kitchen, set a couple of places, lit a candle, and checked for Jodi. There she stood in my bedroom without any clothes on. She was in profile, facing the window. The sun was shining in, casting a yellow pool of light on the green carpet. She stood in the middle of the light, her eyes half-closed as if she were dreaming. Her body was muscular as bright as a copper penny. The back of her arms and legs were in shadow, her rear end like the dark side of the moon. Her breasts were miniature suns, her nipples bright red sunspots. I noticed that my bed was turned down. Jodi turned toward me, opened her eyes, and smiled sweetly.

Prospect Street, Gloucester

I am sitting at the picnic table in front of the food stand that says "Take ove C v." I am eating a cheese-filled pierogi.

I can feel Jodi's hand on my knee. She leans close to me, her hand moving up my leg to the crotch, under the table where no one can see. "I can't get enough of you," she whispers in my ear.

Only she's not there. I am imagining her in my head. It's like the picture, only it isn't real. Maybe the picture isn't real. Maybe it changes. One day I am driving by the very spot on my way to work when I see the shirtless man and his two friends at the picnic table. Between the man and his friend with the ponytail, Jodi is sitting. She is laughing. She is holding the man's hand. She is not in the car. Her hair does not scatter in thin tendrils that curl around her face. I do not see her profile. I see her at the table holding the man's hand. What is this, an episode from *The Twilight Zone*?

I confront her with what I have seen, and she tells me that I do not own her. She tells me a story. "I grew up in Gloucester, Massachusetts, on Prospect Street," Jodi begins. "In a block of big houses on a hill that overlooked the ocean."

"You're like the kids at my high school," I gripe. "You live in a house like I always wanted to live in."

"Be quiet. This is my story," she says. She is sitting at the kitchen table in my apartment. We are eating dinner. "My father was a banker. My mother was a lawyer, though there wasn't much business in a fishing town. So she stayed home most of the time. I had the perfect family, a brother and a sister. I was especially close to my sister, who was a year younger than me. We did everything together. We went to the movies. We went to the mall. We played soccer on the same team, though she was much better than me. They called us the Olsen twins. My hair was blond then. Well, dirty blond. So was hers, though her nose was straight. I have a little bump on my nose."

She turns her head sideways so I can see it—a barely perceptible bump where the angle of her nose changed no more than a degree. "That's beautiful," I say. I love small imperfections. They somehow define a person better.

"Quiet," she says. "Marion was a better student than I. She got straight As, but I wasn't jealous, because I loved her so much and there was so much we shared in common. The one thing we loved the best was to sit in the window seat in the front of the house and look across the street. There were no houses or trees on the other side. There was a sidewalk that led downhill to our school, but other than that, the view was unobstructed all the way down the hill to the ocean. You could see for miles. We had a pair of binoculars that we shared. We weren't looking for the fishing boats that came and went all hours of the day and night. We were looking for the big boats, miles out there. They steamed over the horizon like silent ghosts moving toward us until a few miles out, they turned south toward Boston and New York. Tankers, container ships, tramp steamers. Cruise ships. We saw the *Queen Elizabeth*, the *Queen Mary*, the *France*.

"Marion wanted to travel on a tramp steamer. She'd sail across the ocean to Paris, where she'd live on the Left Bank in a cheap garret room. She'd paint. She'd become famous, show in all the galleries in Paris, London, and New York. She'd marry a fellow artist, and they'd devote the rest of their lives to their art and to the passion they had for each other. I, on the other hand, would sail across the ocean on the *France*, move to the Côte d'Azur, where I'd meet a baron. We'd sail from island to island in a yacht like Jackie Onassis. We'd get married. Have children. Maybe. I was less definite about my plans than Marion. Ever since she could lift a pencil, she was a drawer. She was very determined. I had the sense that her dreams were not as far off as my own.

"One day I was sitting in the window seat looking out the big window. It was an early afternoon in spring. A breeze was blowing in from the ocean. I could smell the salt air. I couldn't see much because a fog bank was moving in like a wall of tundra out over the ocean, but I didn't care. I was waiting for Marion, who was coming home from school. I had been sick that day and bored to death. Across the street, our neighbor parked his car, a big, ugly green thing with a canvas top.

"I couldn't see Marion as she came up the sidewalk, but then there she was, standing in front of the car, one hand holding the rucksack that was slung over her shoulder, the other waving at me. She stepped out in the street, and out of the side of my eye, I could see a red pickup barreling around the corner to my right. I don't think Marion saw the pickup, and I know the driver didn't see her, because he didn't brake until after impact. The bumper must've caught her low, because she flew up in the air. She banged her head against the windshield."

Jodi slumps forward. She covers her eyes.

I listen to her whimper for a few minutes. I pat her shoulder. "What happened?" I ask softly.

"Marion died instantly."

"That's awful," I say. "Why did you want to tell me that story?"

White Castle

I hate pierogies. I hate Jodi, though I think about her all the time. I drive by the fast-food stand on my way to and from work. Sometimes I see the man with the long hair

51

by himself sitting at the picnic table. Sometimes I see him with Jodi. Sometimes I see him with his friends and Jodi. Sometimes with his friends like I saw him at first, but never is Jodi inside the cab of my truck as she was at first.

One day I see the ponytailed man sitting alone at the picnic table inhaling a pierogi. I park the pickup and saunter up to him in a nonchalant manner. I ask him what are the intentions of his friend as far as Jodi is concerned.

He halts mid-bite and looks at me with a jaundiced eye. "That boy doesn't have any intentions I know of."

I think about this but am not sure what he means.

On the way to work the next day, I see them strolling down the street holding hands. Then I glimpse them kissing in the park where I go to eat lunch. Once I follow the man home, and there she is, sitting on the steps of his house. I am hiding behind a tree across the street. I watch them laugh. I watch her grab his belt and pull him toward her. They kiss. They go inside. They go upstairs. They pull down the shade. They turn on the light. I watch their silhouettes on the shade. I run away and tell myself there are other women that I can find.

I go to a couple of bars to see if the other women are there. They are, women who seem approachable, but I don't approach them. I am too busy thinking of Jodi and how much she means to me. I think of our stories. I understand how bad she must feel to have lost her sister: to have actually watched Marion as she crossed the street in the path of a pickup, to have watched her whack her head against the windshield and be unable to do anything. I imagine the blood all over the place, the blank look in the eyes that no longer see.

I am sitting at the bar staring at myself in the mirror. Tears run down my cheek. The bartender stares at me like I'm crazy. When I ask him for another shot of bourbon, he says, "Go home. Go to sleep. You'll feel better tomorrow."

I take his advice. I walk outside. The sky is black. The buildings are hunched over like cats stalking their prey. A blue PT Cruiser races down the empty street, wheels screeching as it avoids the curb near where I'm sauntering dejectedly. It sprays water on my pants leg and screeches around the corner like a disappearing ghost. I hear the buzz of the streetlamps and look up at the blue light that blinds me. I feel a ghostly presence beside me and jump sideways. It is my reflection in a storefront window jumping sideways. I amble up closer. I am blue: my shirt collar, my neck, my Adam's apple, my eyes, my freckled cheeks down which I see the now-dried stain of my blue tears. I stare at myself. I make faces: a frown, a laugh, a gape, and a thousand-yard stare. And suddenly, reflected in those blue eyes, I see the experience that I have gone through with Jodi. And just as suddenly, like a flash out of the blue, I understand her story.

What I do next is that a few days later I see Jodi across the street. I say hello. She says hello, but I can tell that she's uncomfortable, the way she shifts her eyes away from me. She stares at her feet. I run across the street and say in a tolerant tone, "Hey. How are you?"

"I'm fine," she responds.

"That's good. I'm really glad that you're doing well," I add. "We should see more of each other."

She looks at me askance as if she's wondering what planet I come from.

"I mean, you have a boyfriend and that's fine," I say. "We can still be friends."

"You don't have any hard feelings?" she asks.

"Well, at first I did, but I don't now. Things change, and you got to learn how to live with those changes."

Now she squeezes my hand and says, "Thank you, I'm so glad you understand."

Her boyfriend sees us and rushes across the street.

"Hey," he growls.

I introduce myself. I tell him that I am an old friend of Jodi's, that we haven't seen each other in a long time, and that it was nice to see her now. He puts his arm around her protectively. I smile. We decide to go out to lunch at the fast-food stand.

In the weeks that follow, I see Jodi often. Sometimes I say hello and leave it at that. Other times I go out to the movies or to a club to listen to music with her and the boyfriend. Wilson, the white-haired man, and Jock, the man with the ponytail that I saw at the fast-food stand, often come with us. One time we go to an independent film, *Little Miss Sunshine*, and a bar afterward. The boyfriend and Jock hate the movie.

"Not enough action," says Jock.

A few weeks later we go to a blues festival in the park.

"I hate blues," says the boyfriend. He and Jock leave in the middle of the first band.

"I guess you and your boyfriend don't share much in common," I say to Jodi one night at a corner café. We've been talking for hours and hours, mostly about him, the long-haired, bare-chested creep.

"Opposites attract," she says, but I can tell she doesn't believe that.

Summer Interior

I head to her apartment on the other side of the park. Down the path overhung by tree branches that are so heavily freighted by leaves it is like going through a dark tunnel. It is a hot summer day.

I emerge on the other side, cross the street to her brownstone, and clomp up the stairs. I knock on her door. No one answers. At first I think it is because she isn't home. But then I see a light coming through the transom window. I try the doorknob. The door creaks open. I step in the hallway, close the door behind me. I call her name. I hear a sigh but no answer. I creep forward slowly. She lives in a one-room apartment. The walls are painted an ocher color; the carpet is green. At the far end of the room is a white marble fireplace. On either side of the mantelpiece are gold candlesticks, and in the middle, an old-fashioned wood clock that chimes on the hour. It is doing that now, one, two, three o'clock. The fireplace is partially blocked by the footboard of her bed. The bed is wood—mahogany, I think. At the foot of the bed is an orange blanket with red stripes. The white sheet is half on the bed. She is sitting on the floor on the other half of the sheet. She is looking down so I can see the top of her head. Her hair is in a bun. She is wearing a white blouse and nothing else.

"Are you okay?" I ask her. She shakes her head. I want to reach down and grab her in my arms. I want to put her on the bed and make love to her, but I know this is not the right time. I know exactly what has happened.

Fast Food

The wind is blowing in the driver's-side window. It scatters her hair, thin brown tendrils like tiny snakes that curl around her face. Her lips are covered in a shiny neutral gloss that makes them seem wet. Jodi is in profile. I see only one eye. It is blue. It stares straight ahead down the highway. I think she is pensive, like she is wondering what will happen next.

Beyond her profile, I see the dirty window. It is hard to make out what is on the other side of the window. Three men sitting at a picnic table. The one facing me has his hand raised as though he's making a point. He is shirtless. He has long hair and a mustache; the look in his eye is sinister. I know exactly what he is thinking. I laugh. Jodi laughs with me as we squeal down the highway, leaving the fast-food stand behind us forever.

Happiness

I KNOW I SHOULD HAVE A LIFE OF MY OWN, AND I WOULD IF my life wasn't tangled up with hers.

"You don't pay enough attention to me," she complained a thousand times during our marriage. There was a reason for that. Savannah begged me to buy her a house in Coconut Grove, a midcentury ranch with lots of windows and skylights to let in the sun and a swimming pool out back. It cost a fortune. I worked day and night at my shop in South Beach to pay the mortgage. But in the end, she couldn't handle it.

It's Father's Day. The first one after the divorce. I have the boys. They are clones of their mom. Curly golden hair down to their shoulders. Light-blue eyes. Skinny. Muscular. Flat stomachs. Their mother is the most beautiful woman I've ever seen. Like she was born out of my dreams.

My name is Samuel. I'm the anomaly in this family, a skinny, knobby-kneed Jew with poor eyesight and a receding hairline. I was raised in northeast Philly by my grandma. Her advice after I finished Temple University was that "we move to somewhere where the dead don't walk the streets," her reference to the excessive number of graveyards in the

Northeast and to my mother. She died when I was two. I don't remember her.

We moved to South Beach. It felt weird living with Grandma. She was old school, immigrated to the US when she was fourteen from Kraków, Poland. She called me *boytshik*. She died within a year, and it felt weirder. I had a huge hole in my heart. I turned to alcohol. Then I went into rehab, and that was where I met Savannah.

Savannah grew up in Ohio. "I was the prettiest girl in town," she said. "All the boys liked me." But then she left town for San Francisco when her parents divorced. They were old hippies, and she retained some of the old hippie ways. She took up exotic dancing. Most of her customers were Japanese businessmen. Then she moved to the Caribbean where she didn't tell me what she did other than crew on sailing yachts. Finally she washed ashore in South Beach, lonely and bereft like me. I think the moment I fell in love with her was when I told her about Grandma and she started to call me *boytshik*. Still does, though now, I think, more in jest than an endearment.

I stagger into the living room, yawning after a fitful night of sleep agonizing over my ex and her rich boyfriend. Steele and Sage are constructing a rocket out of Tinkertoys.

"Hi, Dad," they say in unison. They look so much alike. They could almost be twins, though they are a year apart. Sage is eight; Steele, seven. We are the *S* family: Savannah, Samuel, Sage, and Steele. Savannah's idea. I think Steele is the straw that broke the camel's back.

"One child is enough," she said at one time. "Two would be fine if you were around."

I pour two bowls of granola and milk, two orange juices, and coffee for myself. The boys sit at the kitchen table reading comic books while they eat. I sit in front of the computer staring out at the ocean beyond Ocean Drive. When we got divorced, I sold the Coconut Grove house and purchased two condos, one for myself, the other for Savannah. She doesn't like that I live in the same building as her though on a different floor. She thinks divorced men should live in cramped studio apartments. Sacrifice for the family. But my business is doing so well that I don't have to sacrifice. Besides, I don't want to disrupt the boys' life. Our condos are almost exactly alike.

I click on Savannah's Facebook page. This is an obsession with me to see what she posts next. The first is a post from her that says, "Life is full of actions! I am a true believer of walking your talk. One of the things I talk about is, love is winning and I must cultivate the goddess in me. Grateful to be embodying my best life! So much good happening in my life right now! Just wow!"

I know the good happening in her life is Roger van Pelt, her hunky yoga instructor. I see her almost every day in the park across Ocean Drive with Roger, twisting her body like a pretzel. She is one of his best students.

I don't want to think about it. Not that I hate her boyfriend. When I came to the door on Friday to pick up the boys—Savannah has custody during the week—Roger was there to greet me. He asked me how my business was doing and if I have any prospects. I think he is jealous of me. He may be a hunk, but he is also as smitten with Savannah as I am. The funny thing is that I introduced them. Roger owns the yoga studio above my store, another one in Fort Lauderdale, and a third in Boca Raton. I feel sorry for Roger because, you know, she might get bored with him. She did once before and threw him out. But he came crawling back. That's the goddess in her.

"I love myself unconditionally," she says in another one of her posts. "I am sovereign, I am healthy, and I am free, and anyone who tells me otherwise can, well...fuck off."

I don't know why she told Roger to fuck off. But she did, like she did me. I imagine it's boredom. But it's something else that I can totally relate to. I mean, it's why we were so compatible at first.

I think the happiest day of my life was when I pulled in the driveway of our house in Coconut Grove in a 1957 baby-blue-and-white Chevy Bel Air convertible. Savannah had been hinting about buying a midcentury car to match our midcentury house, so I decided to surprise her.

I opened the back gate. Savannah was sunning herself in a lounge chair. Sage slept in his cradle shaded by one of the palm trees that lined our long, skinny pool that reminded me of the pool at the Delano hotel, even had a fountain in the middle, spouting water. She turned her head, shaded her eyes, and smiled. "Hi, you're home early."

"I brought something for you," I said. She followed me out of the gate, and when she saw the Bel Air, she leaped up in the air like a cheerleader. "Hooray!" she yelled.

She threw her arms over my shoulders and pecked me on the cheek.

"I love you. I love you," she cooed, pecking me on the cheek again and again. She circled the car, her flip-flops slapping the pavement.

"Oh, oh, it's so beautiful," she gushed as she jumped behind the wheel. "Let's take it for a spin."

"Not yet. You get dressed. I'm taking you to dinner."

She dashed in the house. I wandered back to the pool and scooped up Sage. He was the calmest baby, awoke only once a night at two a.m. for his feeding and again at six when I fed him a bottle before I went off to work.

The babysitter rang the doorbell. I grabbed a bottle of sparkling grape juice from the fridge, and we jumped in the Chevy. She turned on the engine. "Oh, it purrs like a kitten," she said.

We drove down A1A with the top down, past the highrises to Mabel's Seafood Shack, a restaurant on stilts overlooking the ocean. We sat on the deck. Watched the yachts and sailboats chug up the channel as the sun set behind us, turning the ocean a golden color, the wave tips pink. The waiter poured the bubbly.

"I wish it was real champagne." Savannah sighed.

"So do I," I said. It was difficult being a dry drunk, one

of the reasons Savannah was fixated by the goddess idea. Sometimes on Facebook, she would post pictures of super-heroes like Wonder Woman. I knew why. I felt the same way.

After dinner, we took a long walk on the beach. It was a dark night, and far out in the ocean, we could see flashes of lightning light up the clouds. Savannah clung to me tightly and whispered, "If you could wish for anything, what would it be?"

"Oh, I don't know," I said, thinking. "Maybe I wish that our mortgage magically disappeared and we owned the house outright."

She tugged at my shoulder. "Anything else."

"That you're pregnant."

"I'm pregnant." She laughed.

Now it was my time to leap up in the air like a cheer-leader and shout hooray.

Later that night in bed, she curled up to me and whispered in my ear, "I love you, my *boytshik*. I love you." She squeezed my hand. "I need you so-o-o much." This was the happiest moment of my life to know that I was needed, to know that I was loved. I walked down the beach with love. Love drove me home to our house and whispered in my ear before I slept.

So it's Father's Day, and Savannah promised to come to my condo. She purchased a gift, she said, for the father of her children.

I scroll down Savannah's Facebook page to a photograph of Bill Gates. The caption reads, "Baby Killer." Savannah is anti-vax. She believes that the body can heal itself.

I told her of a neighbor in northeast Philly confined to a wheelchair because of polio. The vaccine would've saved her.

"The vaccine could've killed her. She's lucky to be in a wheelchair."

"What do you mean by that?"

"I mean the Gates Foundation tested a polio vax in India that paralyzed four hundred and ninety-six thousand children, and I don't know how many died."

When Steele was born two months premature, I insisted on vaccinations. He was in an Isolette so long, he was like a hothouse flower. Savannah threw a fit.

"I can't live with a man who doesn't give a damn for my passions," she insisted, poking her chest. "I need the support of my fellow warriors." She meant her Facebook friends. She had a couple thousand, most of whom supported her; the others who didn't she called haters. There seemed fewer and fewer of the haters commenting on her posts.

One day when Steele was five, Savannah picked up the boys at the shop and rushed down the street to a Ford Skyliner parked in front of Jimmy Bottom's art gallery. She marched into the gallery. The boys dawdled outside. I kept an eye on them. Cars cruised bumper to bumper up and down Ocean Drive. The occupants gawked at the art deco storefronts, the restaurants, and the gaudily dressed local eccentrics strolling along, their bichons and Yorkies in tow. Steele paid no attention to these dogs. He seemed to eye a basset hound on the other side of the street. He stepped off the curb.

I hustled up and grabbed his hand. "Please, Daddy," he said. I grabbed Sage with my other hand, and we crossed at a crosswalk. The boys ran up and hugged the basset.

Steele looked at me. "I want a doggy, Daddy." He had asked for a dog before, but his mom wouldn't allow it until he was old enough to take care of it himself.

Savannah strolled out of the gallery, a satisfied smile on her face. She bounced a set of keys in her hands. Then she did a double take as if she'd forgotten something, and looked up and down the street and then across at us. Her smile broadened. She dangled the keys between her thumb and forefinger.

When we got back across the street, she put the boys in the back seat of the Ford and jumped behind the steering wheel. "Watch this," she said.

She turned over the engine, unlatched the top, and pushed a button. The trunk opened up and swallowed the hardtop, then closed. "A convertible," she said, smiling triumphantly. "Jimmy and I agreed that I could drive his car around and he could use the Bel Air. Then, if I liked the Ford, we could exchange."

When I reached home that night, Savannah and Steele were arguing.

"I want a doggy," whined Steele. "Please, please, please."

"You can't have a dog until you're old enough to take care of it," hissed Savannah.

"I'm old enough, Mommy," whispered Sage. "I can take care of a dog."

"No, you can't." She turned to me. "All day Steele says, 'I want a doggy. I want a doggy.' It's driving me nuts." She put her hands to her ears and rocked her head from side to side in exasperation. "Now Sage wants a doggy."

"Well, maybe you should get them one."

Savannah raised her hands in the air as if she was appealing to her fellow warriors and screamed. She rushed into our bedroom and slammed the door. The boys and I ate dinner alone. I put them to bed, and when I tiptoed into our bedroom, Savannah was at the computer sharing a message on her Facebook page.

"All You Need Is Love," she commented on the share—photographs of Bill Gates, George Soros, Henry Kissinger, and Jacob Rothschild that seemed to be floating down in a breath of wind to an ocean full of hearts. Underneath was the caption in red letters: "New World Order drowned by love."

"I can understand Bill Gates," I said, looking over her shoulder, "but the rest of these people are Jewish. Are you suggesting Jews run the world?"

"The corrupt politicians and capitalists run the world. Some are Jewish."

"Sounds like hate speech to me. Neo-Nazi propaganda."

"I'm not a Nazi, and I don't hate anyone," she swiveled around in her chair and looked up at me with narrowed, catlike eyes as though she was going to pounce. "I choose love over fear and hate. I love myself. I love those who love me. You don't understand that I am a goddess, I am healthy, and I am free. I don't care what you think. I will speak my truth because I know in my gut that I am right."

I spent the night with the boys. The next morning the Ford Skyliner was gone. I waited a week until Savannah returned from Ohio, where she was commiserating with her mom. She asked for a divorce.

So it's Father's Day, and Savannah shows up with a Longines twelve-karat gold art deco wristwatch. "A gift from Roger and me," she says.

"Gee, thanks."

She smiles, pats me on the shoulder. "A goodbye gift."

"Where are you going?"

"Nowhere. Roger and I plan to get married. Then we're going to go on a long honeymoon to Europe. You'll take care of the kids while we're gone, won't you?"

The next three days, I am in a daze. I fall off the wagon. I drink too many mojitos in the bar at the Penguin Hotel. I carouse with the regulars, one of whom is Jimmy Bottoms.

"I'm lonely because I don't have a partner," he says, gnawing on the sugarcane stick in his mojito. "You're lonely because you do."

"Not anymore."

"Oh yeah, that's right," he says, snickering.

The fourth night I recover my equilibrium. I skip the Penguin Hotel bar. I fix a pastrami sandwich with dill pickle, potato chips, and a glass of sparkling grape juice. I sit in front of the computer looking out at the ocean beyond Ocean Drive. I watch Roger van Pelt playing with the boys on a jungle gym in the park while Savannah twists her body like a pretzel. I click on her Facebook page, and the first thing I see is George Soros. He is, according to the caption, funding the invasions of small-town America by busloads of armed antifa.

"Didn't the antifa storm the beaches at Normandy?" I once asked her. She didn't have the slightest clue what I was talking about, nor would she ever, even if I explain it to her. A childhood memory pops into my head out of nowhere.

I remember Christmas in northeast Philly. We received holiday cards. Grandma would hang them on a long string over the fireplace. Then we'd buy a Christmas tree at the local Sinclair gas station. It didn't matter that we were Jewish. We'd decorate the tree and enjoy it for a while. If the snow came, we'd build a snowman. But then the snow melted. We threw the tree in the yard. The trash man picked it up. It was sad when the season was over, but then we'd have new things to go on to. That's the way I feel right now.

I scroll down Savannah's Facebook page to a drawing of a beautiful long-haired blond woman holding a flaming goblet over her head. "I am the Goddess Peace Ambassador," she says. "I am here to purify the waters of the earth. I play the Zither's melody. I am unafraid because I know Love has already Won! Society will continue to crumble…"

I look up from the page to the park across the street. Roger is sitting on the bench with his arms around Sage and Steele. They stare at my ex-wife as if waiting impatiently for her to end her yoga contortions.

I look back down at Savannah's Facebook page. I guess I don't have any hard feelings anymore, but for my own sanity, I scroll to the top of the page, click on the person figure, and at the bottom of drop-down menu, I click on "Unfriend."

Hallelujah

THE NUMBER ONE RULE OF THE ROAD IS THAT THE LONGER you wait for a ride, the longer the distance it will take you. We're on the last pass in the Sierra Nevadas. We ate the last of the gorp. We shared the last Granny Smith, and now we're sharing the final contents of my canteen, cherry Kool-Aid mixed with vodka. The air is thin. It's hard to breathe. The cars rumble by slowly, but none of them stop. We've been waiting two hours—Jack, my roommate from college; Penny, a beautiful stranger we met along the road; and I.

We've been eyeing a hole behind us, four feet deep. Dirt, rocks, and an empty Pepsi can. We know that it's totally against the rules, but we're desperate. Jack and I duck down in the hole so we can't be seen from the road. Penny giggles. She sticks out her thumb. The cars rumble by, but within a minute we hear the screech of brakes. We peer over the hole. Penny is at the window of a beat-up International Harvester pickup, Depression-era vintage. We see two blond, curly-haired bobbing heads behind the glass. Penny waves in our direction. We emerge from our hole. One of the heads leans out the window. "A couple of jokers," he yells. He motions us to the back. We open a door to a corrugated metal cabin that sits on top of the truck bed.

A wood bench lines each side of the interior. We see four pairs of eyes and hear one disembodied voice intone, "Hey, man."

We climb in. Penny is in the front between the two men. One of them puts his arm around her shoulder. She takes it away. He puts it back.

"Hey, how far you going?" Jack asks the driver.

We pull over the rough gravel to the road.

"Denver."

"That's how far we're going." Jack pokes me in the side.

"But we're stopping off in Reno. These guys don't have money for gas," says Penny, "so I'm going to try to win it for them." Penny has twenty promotional cards worth five dollars each at the casinos. She also promises to take us to dinner.

"Take your arm from around my shoulder," she says.

"Yeah, you letch," says the driver. His name is Kelvin. The letch is Kurt. They're brothers and look exactly alike.

"But we're not twins," says Kurt. "My dick's a foot longer than his."

I'm thinking of my mother way back east in Washington, DC. When we arrive in Denver, Jack and I will pick up the Mustang convertible my parents gave me for Christmas my sophomore year in college. We'll drive back east and stay with Mom for a month. We're going to help her move out of the house on Macomb and move to the Cathedral Apartments on Wisconsin. She'll pay us a thousand dollars each. She doesn't need to do this. She has movers doing most of the heavy work. She knows we're out of money.

I have the sweetest, kindest mother on the face of the earth. The day after my dad's funeral, a couple of friends and I raided the bar and smoked a few joints in the basement rec room. I came upstairs to see how Mom was doing. She was with my dad's fiercely loyal secretary, who took one look at me and said I was a disgrace.

"Don't criticize Bobby," said Mom. "He's very sad about his father."

I was sad. I loved Dad. I postponed my plans for a year after I graduated from college while my friends were out west having fun. I did it because I wanted to be with him. I appreciate Mom's defense of me, but Sandy was right. I am a disgrace.

We pile through the glass doors of the casino in Reno and head off in all directions. Jack and I play the slots. We lose the three quarters we have between us in a matter of seconds. Two casino guards tap us on the shoulder. They are dressed in blue suits and cowboy hats. They escort us to the door.

"Don't ever come back," they say.

Kelvin and Kurt lean against the International Harvester a few feet away. "So they threw you jokers out too?"

Then Tiny, who was squeezed next to us in the back of the pickup—he must weigh 250 pounds—shuffles out the door followed by more cowboys who deliver the same message to him as they did to Jack and me.

Then come the Three Stooges, as they call themselves, three friends from Winnetka, Illinois. One of them asks, "Isn't our money as good as anyone else's?"

"What money?" answers Kurt.

We sit around the parking lot for an hour, the cowboys eyeing us through the glass doors, until Penny emerges waving a wad of bills.

"Hallelujah," she says.

Kelvin climbs behind the wheel of the truck and commands us to push. "You got to jump-start this heap," he says.

The truck hiccups down the road one hundred yards. The engine catches. We jump in.

I'm in love with Penny. She sits across from me in the back, glad to be away from Kurt. Our knees touch as we bounce down the highway. Penny fed us and filled up the gas tank. She spent most of her money, but I know she's happy. We promised to drive her from Denver all the way to Washington. Then she'll take the train up to Philly where she lives. I used to live in Mount Airy on Gowen Avenue. She lives a few streets up on Springfield. We were hitchhiking on this long road in Berkeley where there were about a thousand other people hitchhiking, so it was a long wait and we got to talking. We found out that we knew some people in common and that we'd gone to the same kindergarten together and had the same teacher, though we don't remember each other. I moved to DC when I was nine years old.

I don't know why I love Penny. She's a rough girl like Calamity Jane. She's dressed in motorcycle boots, torn jeans, and a fringed shirt. She has a round face that comes to a point at her chin; big brown doe eyes; thick, sensuous lips; and large breasts. At dinner, she drank three beers. She burped maybe six or eight times, so loud once it woke up Kelvin, who was tired from driving.

So I'm sitting there talking to Penny above the roar of the engine and the whir of the tires against the bumpy macadam road. She says that her last name is Kenny. Penny Kenny. Her father's a judge and a drunk. Her mother's a pussycat. "I'm not going to be a pussycat. I'm not going to let anyone run roughshod over me."

I tell Penny that my father died. She tells me how sorry she is. I say he was a nice guy. He had a great sense of humor. Once he dressed up like a pumpkin on Halloween. There's an edge to my voice. I can feel the tears welling up in my eyes, but it's dark in back of the truck, so she can't see well, I think.

I change places with one of the Three Stooges. I put my arm around Penny. Kurt, who's not driving, yells from the front that we are headed through the night. We're going to drive and drive, up the mountains, down the mountains, across the deserts, through Salt Lake until we reach Denver. It can take seventeen hours, but he has to get home quick. Both he and Kelvin have job interviews.

I fall asleep and dream that I'm about six years old at a horse show in the country in a big crowd and I'm scared. I'm all alone. I scan the crowd, but I don't recognize anyone, a bunch of horsey men and women in jodhpurs and felt hats. Nasty looks on their faces. Then I hear a familiar cough. Mom. She's a smoker. I hear it in the distance, moving closer. The crowd parts. She walks up, leans down to where I'm sitting on the ground. She hugs me. I wake up.

The International Harvester is parked by the side of the road. Kelvin peers in the back door, holding a ten-gallon gas can.

"I'm getting gas," he says. "You jokers wait here."

He saunters off, casually smoking a cigarette. He slides down a gully and reappears on the other side, climbing a hill. He throws the gas can over a barbed-wire fence, parts the wires, and slips through gingerly. At the top of the hill is a house with a porch light on, and about a hundred yards off, a huge tank. Kelvin emerges from the shadows near the tank. He puts down the gas can, stamps out his cigarette, and dives to the ground.

A police car pulls up behind us. A cop slides out the driver's side and saunters up to us, hitching his pants.

He shines a flashlight in our faces and then on the patch at his shoulder. It says "Ute Reservation Police."

"I been working for two weeks," he says proudly. He's a kid. A patch of black hair, shiny black eyes, and a big smile that expose his pearly white teeth.

Two more police cars pull up behind the first. Four cops pile out. They're dressed in blue uniforms and cowboy hats like the casino guards.

"They're from the state police," says the kid. He's dressed in tan. "In case I need backup."

"Backup for what?" asks Kurt. "We're no trouble."

"That depends," says one of the cowboys, the one with stripes on his shoulder as he walks up, "whether you been stealing gas or not like the lady in the house told us." He points up the hill. The lady stands under the porch light shading her eyes, staring down at us.

Two of the cops head up the hill to talk to her. They search around the house. They search around the tank. They blend into the shadows of the hill and a few minutes later come out on this side of the gully holding a gas can.

"There's nobody up there," says one of the cowboys. "But we found this. It's empty."

They wander off to their cars to consult leaving the Ute kid behind to guard us. He smiles gingerly at us and tucks his thumb in his belt near the gun holster. The cowboys wander back.

"An empty gas can isn't evidence," says the policeman with the stripes, "so I guess we got to let you go as much as I don't want to. There's too many of you. We don't want to start a revolution." He smiles at his buddies.

"We're going to have to jump-start the truck," says Kurt.

"Okay," says the cop. We lean our shoulders into the back of the truck and push. The truck hiccups down the road. The engine catches. We jump in.

The cop saunters over to the driver's-side window and leans in. "I want you to get off the Ute Reservation as fast as you can and out of the state of Utah. I don't want you to ever come back again."

We trundle down the road in fits and starts. "We got no more than ten miles of gas," Kurt whines. "What are we going to do?"

We roll into a sleepy Indian reservation town. A few abode huts, dilapidated wood shacks, and a brand-new gas station and grocery store, open twenty-four hours.

"I still have twenty bucks left over from the casino," says Penny.

"Why didn't you tell us that before?"

"You never asked."

Kurt laughs and shakes his head. "Poor Kelvin," he says.

We buy fifteen gallons of gas and two bags of groceries. We pull the truck out to the road. It hiccups for a few yards. The engine catches. We jump in.

Penny is in the front seat between Kurt and one of the Stooges. I can see her ponytail bob from side to side as we shimmy down the road. Kurt leans over and whispers to her, words I cannot hear above the roar of the engine and the whir of the road. When we pass a sign that says we are now leaving the Ute Indian Reservation, we pull over at a rest stop. A bunch of picnic tables on a grass plot surrounded by cottonwood trees that block the view from the highway. The wind sways the trees and blows against our faces, a welcome relief after the heat of the day. I can hear the burbling of a nearby brook.

Kurt says we're going to wait here. "I know Kelvin," he says. "He's circling around to the highway. He'll hitchhike to where we are."

"That is, if the cops don't catch him," says one of the Stooges. "He's only one revolutionary."

We take the two bags of groceries out of the car and munch idly on the contents while Jack gives us a lesson on the constellations in the night sky. Kurt has trapped Penny over in the shadows of the truck. I think he's talking dirty to her because all of a sudden she lets loose with a couple of foulmouthed oaths. He grabs her breasts. She slaps him. He jumps back out of the shadows, pursued by Penny. She lands a left hook on the tip of his chin. He falls in the bushes, less from the force of the blow than from being knocked off-balance.

He is like a cat. He leaps to his feet and turns toward Penny. He's a thin and wiry guy like his brother. He looks quick. I'm sure he could beat the crap out of her. But he hesitates when we come over.

"Can you believe this girl?" he says, swiping his chin. "I don't think I want her in my truck."

He saunters over to the truck, scrounges around the front until he comes up with Penny's red rucksack. He drops it on the ground. Jack and I take out our own gear.

"We're with her," says Jack.

They jump-start the truck and disappear down the road.

We zip our sleeping bags together and drag them down by the brook near a stand of cottonwood but not too close. We want a view of the night sky. I have never seen so many stars, so thick, it was like clouds of silvery cobwebs covering the earth.

"I guess we're not going to make it all the way to Denver in one ride," says Penny as she climbs in the sleeping bag between Jack and me.

"I'm not surprised," I say. "We cheated. We climbed in that hole."

We lay back for a while and look up at the sky. I see a shooting star on the horizon. Jack sees a tiny light that appears and disappears.

"That's a rocket," he says. "It's turning end on end so that when it turns toward us, the light appears, and when it turns away, it disappears."

Jack is a nerd. He has a bird chest and a mop of curly hair like Garfunkel in Simon and Garfunkel.

We start talking about our families. It is me who starts it because I'm thinking about how my mom was saying I'm not a disgrace. I'm thinking about how she cared for my dad in the last year of his life. He was on one of the first kidney machines. They flew out to the University of Utah Hospital in Salt Lake where the doctor who invented the machine taught her how to operate it. Then they flew home, and every three days she operated the machine up to the very day Dad died.

Now, I'm talking to Penny, and she's telling us that she won't let anyone touch her breasts. She isn't a pussycat. She starts singing that Aretha Franklin song: "R-E-S-P-E-C-T, that's what you give to me."

We all laugh even though it's not that funny. We settle down, yawn, look up at the stars. Behind us are the Sierra

Nevadas. Before us the Wasatch mountains. We are on an oasis in a desert plain like nomads stopping off for the night between one destination and another.

Cool Guitar

I DROP BY U STREET LIQUOR TO PICK UP A CASE OF BEER AND a fifth of whiskey.

"I seen you play gigs around town," says the twerp behind the counter, beaming at me. "You're first-class. When you gonna play again?"

"Never." I put the case on the counter. Ask for the Jack Daniel's.

"Maybe what you need is a new piece." He pulls a 1968 Lake Placid blue Fender Stratocaster from beneath the counter. No amp. No cords. A few nicks on the scratch plate. A worn spot where the strap rubbed against the wood. Otherwise mint condition.

"Cool guitar, yes." He giggles. "Used to belong to my brother. You can have it for two thousand."

"No thanks." But to tell the truth, the Strat stops my heart. Right out of the Jimi Hendrix era. I could imagine him playing "Red House" or "The Star-Spangled Banner" at Woodstock. But what can I do? I'm poor. I pay the twerp the money for the booze.

He says, "Hey, maybe next time."

"Yeah. Sure." I lug the stuff down the street.

I stash the case under the sink in the dump the bitch and I share. Put a few in the freezer to cool. Relax in front of the TV sucking on the bottle of Jack.

"You shouldn't drink so much," she whines at me.

I take off my work clothes and throw them on the floor. Put on a pair of shorts.

"You're such a slob."

I come home early a week later to find Nigel, the ex-boy-friend, a law student at GW, in the kitchen patting her on the shoulder. He sneaks by on occasion even though they haven't been together since she pulled up at my door three years ago in the red Honda Accord her parents gave her when she turned eighteen. Nigel tells Miranda that she's a good person. That she deserves much better than a rat like me. She's leaning her head against the kitchen table, sobbing. Sees me. Jumps up.

"Why, hi there, Nigel," I intone in a friendly voice as I raise my fists and hunch over in a fighter's stance. "Trying to screw my girlfriend behind my back."

I take a few lazy swings in his direction that he easily dodges. He backs up against a chair. Trips. Staggers to the opposite side of the table. "Don't you touch me. Don't you touch me," he whines in a voice not that much different than Miranda's.

"What are you going to do, sue me?" I cackle as I flush him out. I chase him around the TV a couple of times and out the front door.

I stand on the front stoop, shake my fist, and laugh at the retreating figure.

"You bastard," she growls at me as I slump down in front of the TV with my beer and Jack chaser. She is right. I am a bastard.

I have an attitude. The world is rotten. It's dealt me a bad hand. My mom ran away. My dad raised me. He's an ex-marine. Vietnam era, though the closest he got to Vietnam was Camp Pendleton. He believes in *duty*. He rode my ass all the way through elementary and junior high. I smoked my first joint in sixth grade. By freshman year, I smoked regularly, both joints and butts, and boozed to excess. I hated school. I skipped often. I was suspended twice. I ran away six times.

"What's the matter, son, is that you're angry because the teachers make you do things and I make you do things," said Dad, getting up close to me like a drill sergeant. "You don't think there is anything worth doing other than your own pleasure."

My pleasure is the blues. They have infected me ever since Jimi and Cream entered my consciousness. Like "Strange Brew" led me to Albert King doing "Crosscut Saw." And Cream and Jeff Beck led me to Howlin' Wolf, once I figured out who Chester Burnett was. Ever since I was thirteen and traded my portable typewriter for a beat-up Japanese guitar, I've been in a band. And that's why I'm upset that her ex lurks around like a vulture.

I knock on the bedroom door after I have my fill of liquor and TV. I beg Miranda to let me in.

"I'm not going to after the way you treated Ed," she says. "You know he wasn't going to screw me. He's my friend. I can have friends, can't I?"

"Sure, baby, but your friends got to not call me a rat." I lean against the door. "I love you."

"You don't love me. If you loved me, you'd stop drinking. Go back to your music." That's what attracted her to me in the first place. She saw me play at a gig and fell in love, hook, line, and sinker.

"Please let me in, darling. Lover," I whisper through the locked door. "All I want to do is hold you in my arms."

"Sure. I'll bet." Her resolve breaks down as it always does. The door swings open slowly, and I stagger in. I collapse on the bed and fall asleep.

In the morning, she fixes breakfast. Ham. Eggs. Grits. Biscuit. One cup of coffee after another. We sit at the card table watching the morning news. Train wreck. Fire. Hostage situation. Afghan war. I squeeze her hand. "You look beautiful this morning."

She's in a terry-cloth bathrobe that falls open slightly. I see her cleavage. "Thank you," she says. "Why don't you call in sick today."

"Sure. Yeah." She and I are on the same wavelength. I call George, the chef. I am the evening prep guy. He says he'd cover for me, but only one night. Why don't I tell him to fuck off? I wonder. Why don't I get back to my guitar? Like Miranda wants. Like I want. Deep down. But then I think about the guitar legends. Stevie Ray Vaughan. Buddy Guy. Even Danny Gatton. The best guitarist you never heard of. How can I compete with those virtuosos who can squeeze all the juice out of every note like the guitar is the human voice in all its variations, whereas what you get from me is the dull roar of the ocean breaking against the shore one monosyllabic wave after another? I am afraid that after ten years I'd still be getting those dull roars and I'd be playing to empty houses and then I'd end up in the gutter.

I am sitting on the bed after I call Chef George, thinking about the morning news. Hostage taking. Fire. Train wreck. Me. I quit playing the guitar six months ago. The gigs dried up, though Barry, my bass player, is as enthusiastic as ever. He's threatening to hire a new lead. How rotten the world is. But then in walks Miranda the Beautiful from the bathroom without a stitch of clothes on. I forget everything but the sight of her.

We make love all day with the same wild abandon we made love three years ago when she came to my doorstep. In the evening when the sun sets below the house at the far end of the alley and I hear the car horns blaring on U Street, Miranda tries to cheer me up by reading liner notes. Smokin' Joe Kubek lived in a school bus located in a junkyard in Dallas. Stevie Ray Vaughan never graduated from high school. Howlin' Wolf grew up on a plantation in Mississippi.

You know he wasn't the owner's son. Buddy Guy's career was held back by Leonard Chess of Chess Records because he thought Buddy's novel style was "motherfucking noise."

One time, about five years ago, I was backstage at a club in Toledo knocking off a few licks and Buddy Guy waltzed in. He stood around a few minutes, looked thoughtful, and said, "Hey, kid, you're not half-bad." I about died and went to heaven.

But today I'm not falling for Miranda's sanctimonious shit. "You're no different than these guys," she assures me. "They had their setbacks, but that didn't stop them. They pulled themselves together. So can you."

"Sure, babe," I say, though I'm thinking, What a clown. She doesn't know her ass from a hole in the ground. I roll off the bed. Jump in my clothes.

"I'm going out."

"Why?" she asks in her whiny voice.

"Booze."

I wander down the street feeling like I've been let out of a cage.

I punch in the door at U Street Liquor. The twerp sneers at me.

"Another Rolling Rock?"

"No, a pint of Jack Daniel's." I sneer back.

He reaches behind the counter and pulls up the 1968 Lake Placid blue Fender Stratocaster. "Seventeen fifty. I need to unload this baby or my brother will kill me."

I look at the Strat lying there, all shiny blue like a gift from the Muse, a complex instrument that I can squeeze any sound out of. I sigh.

"Give me the Jack."

When I reach home after swigging half the pint from a brown paper bag, I am so surly that when Miranda complains I've been drinking again, I raise my hand to slap her.

She backs up. Starts crying. Runs in the bedroom and slams the door. I hear the lock click.

I settle down in the easy chair, turn on the TV, curse a blue streak, nurse the rest of the bottle, and fall asleep.

The next evening when I arrive home, Miranda's filling out a job application for Starbucks.

I drag a Rolling Rock out of the fridge, collapse in the easy chair, and watch her. She seems so determined, leaning over the paper, writing carefully in her pinched, tiny scribble.

"They promised me the job," she says, looking up and turning toward me. "It's part-time. What I plan to do is sign up for a few courses at GW. Then enroll full-time next fall."

I snicker. She's almost in as deep a funk as I am.

"You're a lazy slob," she says in a determined tone. Not her usual whine. Tears come to her eyes. "That's why I'm doing this. No one is holding me back."

"Now wait a minute, baby." I put down the brew. I feel this sudden wave of fear in my heart like this woman means business.

"You drink too much. You don't care about your music anymore. You sit here watching television and throwing your clothes all over the place."

"I care about the music," I say. "I care about the music. I'm working hard at that stupid restaurant."

I tell her about the Lake Placid Stratocaster. "If I had an instrument like that, I'd play it every day, and then I'd get good like you wouldn't believe."

She laughs, but the tears are still in her eyes. "The instrument doesn't matter," she says. "It's who's playing it."

I feel like snapping her neck off, but instead I run away for a couple of days. I'm going to break her resolve. I hang out at Barry's apartment until he's sick of my whining about Miranda.

When I return to my place, I can't get in. Miranda changed the lock. I wait on the front steps until she pulls up in the Honda Accord. She opens the door. Inside by the TV are about five boxes, my suitcases, my guitar case, and my amps.

"What's the idea?" I ask her. "You kicking me out of my own apartment?"

"It's either you or me," she says, her jaw set. "I want to make a new life."

"Hey, baby," I plead. I remind her of the good times we had together, the gigs out of town when I took her with me. Once in Virginia Beach, we sipped margaritas on the beach. I licked salt out of her belly button. I remind her of all the shows we went to. The great guitarists. I told her I was seriously going to get back into my music, and I meant it. When I was over at Barry's, we attended a Sonny Landreth concert at the Birchmere. We went backstage where we met Sonny's bass. He said that it took him twenty years to become part of a quality band and that now he was enjoying the fruits of his labors.

"The one who wins," he said, "is the one who's left standing."

"I'm beginning to think that's my problem," I tell Miranda. "I need to knuckle down. Work. Have more patience. Things will fall into place."

I try to drag her back to our bedroom, but she resists.

"I don't love you anymore," she says, tossing me the keys to the Honda. "Here, you borrow my car and take your stuff to Barry's. You'll thank me in the end."

I grab the keys and flop down in the easy chair in front of the television. I cover my face with my hands and would've broken out in tears if it hadn't all of a sudden come to me. What I am going to do?

"Okay. Okay. Maybe, you're right," I say, finally, looking up. "Maybe I'll thank you in the end. I don't know."

I push myself out of the easy chair for the last time, my heart racing at warp speed and my mind full of rage at her obvious rejection. I am so full of conflicting emotions that I can hardly breathe as I stagger outside. Toss my possessions in the back of her car. Head back in. Miranda's back to her Starbucks application. Ignoring me, though the way she scrunches up her body in a defensive posture, I know she's afraid.

I walk right past her without a motion in her direction, head into our bedroom, and lock the door. Cackle under my breath. Pull down the portable file in the closet. Take out the vehicle title. Stuff it in my pocket. Open the door.

"Goodbye, Miranda," I say as I amble past her to the door. She doesn't utter a word, but I know she's sad.

The next morning I sell Miranda's Honda Accord. Saunter down U Street to U Street Liquor. I buy the Lake Placid blue Fender Stratocaster for twelve hundred dollars. I run my hand down the frets, touch the dials, and work the arm up and down.

"This better work," I warn the twerp. "Or I'm gonna come back and break your arms and legs."

I take the guitar to Barry's place, where I hook it up to the amps and play the old songs. "Detroit Iron." "Burford's Bop." The sound rich. Bell-like tones. Barry wanders in the room.

"You're playing again," he gushes. "Hot shit."

"Goddamn right," I say, slapping the guitar. "I'm playing again, but this time I'm not going to quit. This is it, man. We're going to play three hundred gigs a year all over the country so everyone will know who we are. Two or three years down the road, you'll see, we'll be under contract."

"We'll be heroes," says Barry with equal enthusiasm.

"Damn right." We laugh like a couple of maniacs, me thinking about Miranda and how right she is. I am a big fucking miraculous bastard, and I don't care because my daddy's right. There isn't nothing worth doing other than your own pleasure.

The Cook

"ONE THING I CAN'T STAND IS SOMEONE WHO'S GOT WHAT I want," says Carl to Howie Wilson, who doesn't know what he's talking about since this is the first time he met the guy.

He tells Howie his job in the kitchen is to scrape the garbage through a hole in the counter that leads to a garbage can, rinse the dishes until there's not a speck of scum left, stack them in the tray in the washer, pull them out when they're through, and stack them on the shelf behind the stove. He shows him how to do silverware and glasses.

"I don't want you to drink the leftover wine out of the glasses like the last guy."

He tells him that in the evening after the kitchen closes, he's to sweep the floor and mop it, and once a week he needs to clean the walls and under the hood over the stove where all the grease is trapped.

"Even a monkey could do your job."

Carl's the cook. He's fat, uglier than sin, and triple-chinned, with black pig eyes and blue pouches underneath, though he looks strong. His arms are as big as Howie's legs.

"Now, my job," he says, "is the most important job in the whole lodge. I'm no monkey."

Howie found his position through his father's business friend, the mayor of Lubbock, who owns the lion's share of the lodge that is located on a hill overlooking Conchas Lake, thirty miles west of Tucumcari. It is modest, a motel with two wings attached to a central area where the reservation desk is located, a cathedral-ceilinged sitting room with trophies on the wall, off of which is the bar, the dining room, and the kitchen. Around the motel is range land but looks to Howie more like desert, mesquite, brush, an occasional twisted juniper tree, or near the water, cottonwoods. In the distance are the mesas.

Howie can't imagine a more desolate spot, which pleases him because it's the opposite of where he comes from, two thousand miles to the east. His parents offered him three choices: attend summer school to fulfill a senior requirement so he can concentrate on studying for the SATs in the fall, fly with them to Europe to visit his recently married sister and her Belgian husband, or this one, the best choice, because he wants to be a man.

"The most important job," says Carl after the supper rush of the first day when they sit at a table in the screened-in porch, soaked in sweat from the hot kitchen, the fan blowing full force in their faces. While Howie chews on meat loaf smothered in white gravy and green beans cooked in bacon grease—not the most healthful food but undeniably delicious—Carl sips from a gallon jug of ice water he carries with him all day. Even now in the cooler air, the sweat pours off his forehead. He chews on an apple.

"And they don't realize it," he says. "If it wasn't for me, there wouldn't be this many customers."

He runs through the employees: Ed, the manager; Peggy, his young wife, who waits tables—Carl lusts after her. They live in a two-bedroom apartment behind the reservation desk. Olin, who does all the odd jobs, drives the people from the airstrip, and shops for food in town, and that pimply-faced nag, his wife, the waitress, Missy, live in a room in the old wing of the motel, as does one of the two women who clean up the rooms—that's not even a full-time job. The other lives in a trailer in Hooverville below the dam.

"Where do you live?"

"Down there." Carl points to the floor. "In the stink hole below the kitchen where the air doesn't circulate. I was up for your room before I even knew there was a you."

In the evening after the dining room closes at nine, the bar fills up, and the country music from the jukebox drifts in the kitchen where Howie finishes the sweeping and mopping—Hank Williams, Webb Pierce, Bob Wills and the Texas Playboys, Garth Brooks, but one song sticks in his mind, the theme song of the summer, an instrumental, "Westphalia Waltz." It has the one-two-three beat of the waltz with the country twang. It makes him want to dance with the ladies, belly up to the bar with the men, but he's a youngster without the proper identification.

Carl invites him to the stink hole, a low-ceilinged room lit by a swag lamp against which Howie knocks his head, nearly shattering the globe. He sits down on a red plastic banquette and stares at a mushroom that grows out of the cinder-block wall. The only other lamp is in the corner next to the bed and the furnace that heats the central area of the lodge. The lamp, the base of which is a rearing horse with a broken-off snout, doesn't have a lampshade. The bed lacks a box spring, though it does have a wafer-thin mattress that reminds him of a camp bed. Carl hands him a Coors from a cooler behind the furnace.

"Would you stand for treatment like this, rich boy?" he says.

The stench of the stink hole is elusive, moist, unlike the desert outside, like a root cellar gone to seed. The smells in the kitchen settle down here. A thin layer of grease sticks to the walls and floor.

"When I was your age, I joined the navy to see the world," says Carl. "I saw the galley instead. Rose from the bottom ranks to chef. Chief chef. They wanted me in submarine service, where they serve the best food. But I didn't want to be closed in. I liked the nights after dinner on the fantail when I felt the salt air soak through my pores and enjoyed all the colors of the sunset. I liked shore leave. Back then I was lean, muscular, hot-looking. One time, out in San Diego, I banged a captain. She was late back to duty but couldn't have cared less. I should've stayed in the service. They didn't put me in no stink hole."

Howie can tell that no one at the lodge cares for Carl, especially Ed. "I have to deal with his constant demands. Either he wants a raise or to move up with us. Since the mayor brought me here four years ago, the cook slept in the basement. He's the best one we've had, attracts plenty of business, but in the end, he creates too much conflict."

Peggy doesn't like the way he eyes her from the swinging door to the kitchen. He makes lewd remarks to her as she passes by. He either ignores Missy or, when she gets an order wrong, curses her out until she seems ready to throw a plate at him. One time she did. Carl ducked, and it shattered against the shelf behind the stove, nearly toppling a row of freshly washed plates. Olin hates Carl because his wife carries her work problems home with her each night. The others don't see much of him.

Howie senses that Carl feels isolated in the basement while the others are far off in a more desirable part of the lodge. He senses that Carl wants to enlist him as an ally. That won't really work. He's more of a go-between.

On Howie's first day off, Olin takes him to a ranch run by a friend of his. They ride all day long, up and down mesas, through miles of flatland covered with mesquite with the hot sun beating down on them. They herd cattle to a water hole.

On his second day off, Ed takes him to Taos, where he once worked as a radio station manager for the mayor. They see a parade, visit the art galleries, and meet Ed's old friends. They go to a party at a hacienda built in the eighteenth century that's being renovated. It doesn't bother Howie that there's a reason that he's treated so well. That Olin complains about how the lodge is run, that he claims that he

could do a better job if given the chance. Nor that Ed complains not only about Carl but also about Olin, how hard
it is isolated out here with ungrateful employees and how
difficult it is to attract customers.

"We're only one of a thousand places to visit in this state,
and most are in more pleasant surroundings. Considering,
I think I do a good job," he says. Howie knows that this information is to get back to the mayor. He senses that they
think he's here to spy on them, which isn't true. He's just
grateful for the experience, to feel at home with people who
come from what he considers an exotic place, to sit out on
the veranda at the back of the lodge and look at the wide-
open spaces he's only seen before in cowboy shows.

His third day off he spends in his room writing letters
to his friends at home, then wanders down the steep hill to
the lake. He hikes around for a few hours and watches the
speedboats pull skiers, the houseboats full of families cruise
up and down the shore, and the swimmers frolic in a roped-
off area. Under a cottonwood tree by the bank, he finds Carl
fishing and nursing a bottle of whiskey. He shares the bottle with Howie. Carl tells him about how when he was on
shore leave in New Caledonia in the South Pacific, he fell
in love with a native girl who was introduced to him by her
mother. He knew the mother had ideas, arranged for an
outrigger to take them to a deserted island in the bay, and
left them there for several days at a hut next to a waterfall
that spilled into a pool you could swim in. "The native girl
was my age, dark-skinned, well endowed, but didn't speak

a word of English. All we did was swim, eat, make love, and drink this native wine that made my head spin."

After his third nip from the whiskey, Howie feels his head also spin. He pictures the scene that Carl paints perfectly in front of him, and somehow it seems familiar.

"We made love under the waterfall, on the ground on top of palm leaves, in a hammock outside the hut, which isn't easy, and the last time on a hill overlooking the battleships and cruisers in the harbor. Her mother wanted me to marry her, even arranged a dowry and native wedding, but I refused her. I returned to my ship late. They tossed me in the brig for a week, but like the captain in San Diego, I felt it was worthwhile. As a matter of fact, I should've married that native lady."

Howie Wilson feels sick. He excuses himself and rushes back to his room, where he collapses on his bed in a leaden sleep. He doesn't awake until the morning.

He stumbles in the kitchen.

"How do you feel?" asks Carl.

"Horrible. My head aches."

"So does mine."

Ed is mad at both of them because they're late for work. He and Howie are forced to do the prep work that Carl usually completes by six a.m. The dishes pile up on the counter, so Peggy gives a hand. Missy's overburdened with too many tables. She screeches her orders to Carl, who covers his ears.

"I can read your scribble," he growls back.

When things calm down, Ed and Peggy leave but not

without a parting shot. "I don't care what you do on your day off," says Ed, "just don't let it affect your work."

"You give me what I deserve," says Carl, "then we'll both be happy."

Howie notices that Carl no longer cares about his cooking. Before, he offered his blue plate special: coq au vin, barbecued ribs Texas style, paella and black bean soup, London broil and Yorkshire pudding, to name a few. Now he offers only the standard fare, fried chicken and mashed potatoes, steak and baked potato, hamburger and fries under- or overcooked depending on his whim.

One night while he mops up after dinner, he hears Ed and Carl arguing in the empty barroom. Ed says that business is slack. Carl counters, "You treat me right, the business returns."

"Don't you try to trick me," fumes Ed. "I do the best that I can."

"So will I once I gain what I deserve, a room upstairs or more money, hardship pay for living in that dungeon that isn't fit for human habitation."

"We've gone over this a thousand times. We have limited funds and space."

"Then you must sacrifice. Move someone else down there."

"I can't do that."

A customer comes in the bar.

Howie feels like less of a go-between. "You can share my room."

"No, thanks. I like my privacy." They wrap a towel around a six-pack of Coors and take it to the old wing. Carl pulls a whiskey flask from his pocket, takes a pull from it, and offers some to Howie. He waves it away, nurses a beer the rest of the evening.

His room is farthest away from the central lodge area, with its own private entrance, own bathroom and closet, three large windows, and metal furniture, except for one fur-upholstered easy chair and a double bed.

"You can invite a lady to visit," says Carl in the chair, the blue pouches underneath his eyes accented by the overhead light.

"When I was your age," he says, "nobody bothered me. I remember after the service the first job I found was in New Orleans, where I had a run-in with a maître d' over a Creole lady. Smoky eyes and a nice figure, you know. She dated the guy, but soon as she saw me, that was it. She hung around until she got my attention. The maitre d' was so upset he told the boss I couldn't cook Creole, our specialty, or nothing else. They fired me, and all I could find was a position at a hash house up north on Gentilly.

"I was out with this lady six months later, we run across the guy, and he tells her what a creep I am, how I'm no good at work, and if she stays with me, she'll end up in the trash heap. So I have to challenge him to a fight. He's no punk, outweighs me by thirty pounds. But I'm like Rocky Marciano, hard as granite. He delivers one blow after another. I stand my ground until he fags out, lets down his guard. Then it's my turn. I knock him to the ropes in a matter of seconds.

"You know what? I helped him up off the ground. The guy says he's sorry for his lies. I say I am too, that we needed to fight. He hires me back. We're best friends. I don't know what happened to the lady, but right now if I wanted to go down there, he'd give me a job just like that." Carl snaps his fingers. "He owns that restaurant where he was maitre d'. Maybe if I'd stayed there, I'd be his partner."

It's late in the summer, and the weather has turned cool, in the low eighties, 10 to 15 degrees below the normal temperature. Carl says he's cold all the time in his basement room. Every day off, it seems he goes down to Hooverville, buys a fifth and some bait, and heads off to a fishing hole under a cottonwood and drinks himself into oblivion. He causes all kinds of havoc the morning after, and he tells everyone he doesn't care. If they find him so undesirable, then Ed should fire him, but Ed does nothing. He tells Howie in confidence that he's been searching, but he can't find a replacement, that even Carl in this condition is better than nothing.

A few weeks before Howie leaves for school back east, he arrives in the kitchen ten minutes early for the morning meal but can't find Carl. He hears a weak voice far off in the stink hole that begs for help. He feels his way down the greasy cement stairs, trips over a body at the bottom, and sprawls to the floor in a pile of smelly clothes. The voice, still weak, curses him. He switches on the swag lamp.

"I twisted my ankle," whispers Carl. He lies on his back, rocking from side to side, his black eyes lost in animal pain. He grits his teeth. "I been here all night."

It takes all of Howie's strength to sit him up, drag him over to the banquette, and lift him so he's relatively comfortable. He props the damaged ankle on a pillow and finds Carl the gallon jug of ice water. He drains the water and asks for another. "You go get Ed quick as you can."

"How would this make you feel?" he asks Ed when they return. He says in the middle of the night he fell down the stairs in the pitch dark, sprained his ankle and back so badly he couldn't get up. So he yelled at the top his lungs, but since everyone's on the other side of the lodge in their plush rooms, he can't be heard. "You're lucky I have a strong constitution."

"This wouldn't happen if you were sober," says Ed.

"It's my right to do what I want on my day off. If I lived upstairs like everyone else, this wouldn't have happened. We'd both be happy."

Howie drives Carl to a clinic in Tucumcari, and when they return, Carl's ankle wrapped, his back in a brace, he's given a room next to the bar, but it has only one window and no bathroom, and the noise seeps through the walls all night so he can't sleep. He quits the job.

Howie helps him pack his ancient Ford Fairlane station wagon.

"Maybe you should stay longer," he says as he notices the difficulty Carl has getting in the car.

"Not on your life. The sooner I'm out, the better I'll feel."

Ed gives Carl his last paycheck along with severance pay in cash, the way he requested it.

"Changed your tune, huh? Afraid that I'll sue you?"

Ed leaves them alone without saying a word, though Howie can tell the way he retreats hunch-shouldered that's exactly his fear.

"Where you going?" asks Howie.

"To my buddy in New Orleans. He'll take care of me until I'm on my feet. Then I'll help him out until next summer, when I'll visit a friend who runs a lodge in the Ozarks. A big place with a lake, two swimming pools, and all the other conveniences, not like this hole. He'll make me head chef, give me a nice place to live, and plenty of free time. He knows a gold mine when he sees one. Or maybe I'll hire on to one of the rigs in the Gulf. I've done that before. It's like being in the navy, surrounded by water and those pretty sunsets. Nobody'll bother me as long as I do my job. And you know what, you get a week off after two weeks of work. I'll head to shore and raise Cain in some small Creole town. Maybe I'll get some whore pregnant." He laughs at this, but Howie can tell by the tone of his voice that he's only half-serious.

They shake hands. "You're a good friend," says Carl, leaning close so no one can overhear, though there isn't anyone within hearing distance, anyone but Howie Wilson to say goodbye. "I left some beers in the walk-in for you."

"Thanks, Carl. I wish I'd done something for you."

"Don't worry, kid. You've done what you could." He pats Howie on the hand, tells him not to take any wooden nickels, slaps the Ford in gear, and takes off.

It's midnight when Howie finishes mopping the kitchen. "Westphalia Waltz" drifts in from the jukebox, but it doesn't make him want to dance with the ladies. He sneaks out to the walk-in, where he finds a couple of beers hidden behind a box of T-bones. He takes one, slides it in his pocket, and sneaks around the back way to his room. He drags a chair out of the room to the shadows near a cottonwood where he can't be seen, and sits down. He pops open the tab. He takes a long sip.

The moon is past full. It seems to drift along with a long, luminescent line of clouds. Out of one of these clouds, a shooting star appears. He can see the long, smoky trail, the bright light of a dust particle that's burning up in the atmosphere. He feels like he lives within the realm of possibility.

In a few weeks, he will return to Washington. His parents will be there with stories about his sister and her wonderful new Belgian husband. They are partners at a start-up company in Budapest. He will start his senior year in school. He will take the SATs. He will apply to colleges, ask out a date to the senior prom, and then, like his sister, he will leave home.

He stares at the vista before him and thinks of Carl. He's probably in Texas in a motel by the highway, his leg propped up on a pillow, watching TV. He can see the blue light reflect off his face. Poor Carl. Howie Wilson wonders what it would feel like to be forty-eight years old like Carl. He wonders why he thought coming out here would make him feel more like a man when, actually, he is not sure what men are supposed to feel like.

Dude

WHEN FRED PUTNAM FINDS OUT HE AND SALLY CAN'T HAVE
children because his sperms don't have tails, he decides he
needs a change of scenery. He is embarrassed, for one thing,
and when Sally suggests they adopt, he's outraged.

"I don't want second best."

Three days later he calls her from a phone booth outside
a café at the Willard, Kansas, exit off I-70.

"I don't know what's gotten into you," she says in an ex-
asperated tone.

"I'm sorry, but I can't live in the same place forever."

"Yes, you can, if you put your mind to it. You can be perfectly happy."

Fred has spent all his life within two blocks of where
he grew up in Prince George's County, Maryland. When
he graduated from high school, he married Sally and entered government service as a clerk for the US Government
Accountability Office. He's advanced four grades. The only
daring thing he's done in his life was going into debt to
purchase the house where they live. But it's not that daring
since they can easily make the monthly payments.

"I love you, Sally. But I need to find myself." He explains to her that it's fate that he's calling from this particular place because inside the café he found a sign for a ranch hand job. As a child, he used to watch Hopalong Cassidy and Roy Rogers religiously on TV. He even went to western camp in Lancaster County, Pennsylvania, where he learned to rope and ride horses.

"It's like a dream come true," he says. "I'll get that job."

"I spoke to your supervisor over the phone when you left," says Sally. "He says you arranged a three-month leave of absence."

"Sally, can't you hear me?"

"Yes, I hear you, but I can't pretend to understand. All I hope is that you wake up before you lose me and your perfectly good job."

"Please, sweetheart." But Sally is inconsolable, and the operator comes on the line to tell him his time is up.

Fred slides behind the wheel of his blue Vega. Maybe I should turn around and head home, he thinks. He looks in the rearview mirror at a wisp of a mustache growing on his upper lip. He looks at the sign the waitress tore down with instructions to the Wells ranch. "It's been up there five years because they always need ranch hands," she said. It's fate to stop at this very place or, as Sally would call it, God's will. He decides to head north through cow country, endless grassland with flat-top, mesa-like hills in the distance and few trees.

He's disappointed when he arrives at the place because

he expects to find a ranch house surrounded by a white picket fence instead of a two-story Colonial. A standard black French poodle lopes around the side of the house and nuzzles him in the crotch.

A pickup with a horse trailer attached to it pulls up behind him, and a large, ruddy-faced man with a handlebar mustache introduces himself as Mr. Wells, exactly as Fred expected, dressed in cowboy boots and spurs, leather chaps with initials etched in them, jeans and jeans jacket, a cowboy shirt, and felt hat with a coon tail attached to the back of it. Fred says that he wants to hire on as a cowboy.

Mr. Wells says to call him Ross. He ushers him in the house to find cowboy gear, chaps for over his jeans, beat-up boots, a jacket with cotton batting spilling out of a couple of holes, oversized gloves, and a Philadelphia Phillies baseball cap.

They climb in the pickup, the French poodle between them, and drive off.

"You know how to ride a horse?"

Fred tells him about his experience at the Lancaster cowboy camp.

"Some cattle of mine strayed through a fence to a neighbor's property. We need to round them up."

"I can handle that," says Fred.

About seven miles outside of Manhattan, they turn right on a dirt road and drive downhill about fifty yards where Ross stops next to a field of dry corn stalks. "You stay inside, Fife," he tells the dog as they jump out of the cab.

"Fifi," says Fred.

"Yeah. It's kind of a joke."

They back the horses out of the trailer. "This brown one's yours. Peanut," says Ross.

"What kind of name is that for a horse?"

"She's small. So she's a peanut."

They climb on the horses. Fred has to readjust the stirrups several times before he's satisfied. "Let's get our butts in gear," growls Ross. They trot up the hill, trample the dry corn stalks, down another grass-covered hill, follow a creek, and climb the opposite bank where Fred gets caught up in a thicket of small trees. The branches catch at his clothes, scratch his face, and rip off his Phillies cap, though he manages to grab it before it falls to the ground. Ross slides down to the creek followed by Fred, who catches on to a tree limb that snaps back in his face. He holds on for dear life. Peanut walks out from under him, and he's in midair, legs kicking, until the limb bends gently down to the creek. He's ankle-deep in water, but his boots protect him. The cowboy finds this amusing.

Fred mounts up. "Sorry," he says.

"Hey, I enjoyed it," says Ross. They ride about half a mile until they come to the crest of another hill at the bottom of which about a dozen cattle are bunched together. "You go down there, round up those strays, and send them up the hill in this direction along the fence line while I go down by the creek."

Fred watches Ross ride off and waits until he's positioned himself in front of the gap. Then he charges downhill. The cattle scatter. Fred tries forever to push them back in a bunch, but it's useless until Ross lends a hand.

When they finally manage to drive the strays through the gap to the top of another hill where they mix in with a few more head, Fred says, "I'm sorry."

"Don't worry," says the cowboy. "You'll learn. You stay here. I'll search for the rest." He rides off.

Fred feels like a fool but only for a moment. He notices the scenery, hill after hill of wavy grass that stretches off to the horizon and a purple haze where the sun is setting. He gawks around him at the emptiness. Other than him, Peanut, and the cattle, there is no other living thing, no other sound. He doesn't know how to take this.

Ross returns with two calves, points at two poles against the horizon a few hills over, and says, "We'll drive them to my land on the other side of that gate."

They follow the fence line. Fred doesn't make any mistakes. When a cow peels off from the herd, she stops to look at him. He approaches her sideways, and when she doesn't turn back, he heads directly toward her but not too close so she will lose her composure and run up against the other cattle. He notices Ross looks back several times with approval.

When they pass through the gate, he says, "Good job, Fred."

Ross introduces him to the family when they arrive home: Kitty, the wife, and Sky and Dawn, the kids. Strange names, but Fred keeps it to himself. They dine on carrots, asparagus, and lamb shank smothered in hunter sauce, not one-tenth as tasty as Sally's cooking. Ross pours a couple of snifters of cognac after dinner and takes Fred out to the bunkhouse, a room in a garage, newly insulated, with a pot-bellied stove, a bed, a sofa, a table, two chairs, a sink, and a small refrigerator. "Does this mean I'm hired?"

"Yes. There's an outhouse out back," Ross says and leaves.

Fred fetches his things from the Vega. He stokes the fire in the potbelly, unzips his down sleeping bag, and drapes it over the bed. He climbs in a pair of long johns and jumps under the covers. He's a real cowboy, he supposes, though he wants Sally here to keep him warm.

As he lies there in the thin light of the fire watching his breath curl out of his mouth in a cold stream, he recalls Sally's passions: one of her strongest for him and another for her job as an auto mechanic at a dealership on Route 1. She's next in line for shop foreman. It doesn't bother him in the least that she's in a man's job, nor that his friends kid him about it. He is proud of her and a tiny bit jealous of how daring she is.

But her final passion for the Baptist church, he's not sure about. She's always there on Sundays. She's always going on retreats, and several nights a week she attends prayer meetings. She wants to convert Fred.

"My only regret in life," she's told him at least five hundred times over the years, "is that when I die and go to heaven, you won't be there with me."

When they found out about the sperms, Sally wouldn't sleep with him for a week, and then one night, she dragged him off the sofa and back to the marriage bed. She kept him up most of the night and almost seemed happy.

"Hallelujah," she shouted at one point. It was like she was on one of her weekend retreats. That was when she got into the adoption thing, but to Fred it was bad enough he couldn't raise his own.

Fred Putnam turns over on his side and curls up to keep warm as the fire burns down in the potbellied stove. He thinks of how he has as much passion for Sally as she does for him. And it's not only sex. She's a caring human being. And though he doesn't care for this religious stuff—he's a lapsed Catholic—he knows that she would make a wonderful mother.

The next morning Ross Wells wakes up Fred before dawn. Six days in a row he does this. They trudge out to the fields to put in winter wheat. His job is to follow behind the tractor until the rotary blades get gummed up with earth, then jump on the hoe to make it dig deeper. He's afraid that any second he'll be thrown in with the blades. When they scatter the seed, he's on the back of the distributor pouring fifty-pound bags of seed down the funnel.

"How many more fields of this we have to do?" he asks Ross when they've finished the first one, three days into his travail.

"About ten, I think, some bigger, some smaller than this one."

They fence in several acres near the house to increase the feedlot capacity. They dig the postholes with a screw bit attached to the back of the tractor. Grapple the poles in the hole and pack in the gravel and dirt. String the barbed wire from pole to pole. The wire is wrapped around huge spools. Sometimes it snaps back on Fred. Rips his clothes and a few times his skin.

They move the cattle to winter pasture near the house by truck. "I don't get this. I thought you used horses."

"You don't understand the modern ranch," says Ross.

He shows Fred his computers in his office where he keeps the ranch records, even down to infinitesimal details such as a comparison of the different nutrients in cattle feed. "It's cheaper to mix it myself." He shows him the futures market he tracks through a call-up service. "In case I have to sell short."

"Sell what short?" asks Fred.

He's confused by the cowboy business and afraid as winter approaches. For one thing, he's always cold except when he's near the heater in the Wells house. He feels maybe he'll catch pneumonia or lose his toes to frostbite. For another, he nearly breaks his neck in a fall from a windmill, gets butted in the groin by the kids' pet billy goat, and gets run over by a herd of spooked deer that come out of nowhere as he's on his way to the outhouse.

The Lord is trying to wake you up, Fred thinks Sally would inform him about now. It is a cold night after Thanksgiving, and he's in the bunkhouse bed thinking about Sally and his sperms.

They'd been trying to get pregnant for a year before the doctor tested to see if she were at fault. And then they tested him and found out the truth, though he didn't believe it until she shouted, "Hallelujah," and mentioned that word.

"I don't want to raise somebody else's baby," he said.

"Once the baby is with us, it's not somebody's else. It's ours."

"No, it isn't. It's not our blood."

"We are all God's children. We are all the same blood." But the argument was fruitless even when Sally mentioned that Fred was not of the same blood as her yet she loved him as if he were.

That night they abandoned themselves to lovemaking again, and in the morning Sally announced that if she can't adopt a baby, she wanted to adopt a puppy or kitty.

Fred didn't like the idea. But he loved his wife. He said okay.

A few weeks later, he went out drinking with the bachelors at work, a rare occasion, but he was upset. He downed four beers and wandered home. There was Sally sitting on the sofa in the living room with the tan Cocker puppy they adopted at the pet shop. It was after eight.

"Where you been?" she asked.

"Here and there." He stared at the puppy, and then, for some reason, he thought what it would be like ten years from now. The puppy would be a doddering old thing, and maybe there would be a couple more, a mutt from the pound, a miniature poodle, a legion of cats. The place would smell to high heaven, and there'd be newspapers piled in the corner turning yellow. He and Sally would be like the queer old couple that lived at the end of his block when he was growing up. He didn't like that thought. So he grabbed the Cocker puppy from Sally's lap. He wanted to dash its brains against the wall, and he made a motion to do so, but Sally stood up and slapped him in the face.

"Don't you dare," she said.

He put the puppy down and stared at her in disbelief. Her straw-colored hair was up in a bun, the way she kept it at work. She was in her dirty, grease-stained coveralls, her legs spread apart, her hands balled up in a fist like she was about to slug him. She sneered at him as if he were a stranger who'd broken into her home. That made him angrier than a hornet, so he slapped her back and pushed her on the couch. For a moment, he hated Sally and wanted to kill her. Then he woke up as if he'd been in a dream.

Fred Putnam turns over in his bed and stares at the fire that is almost dead in the potbellied stove. He flings off the covers and rushes over to the stove, stuffs in one piece of wood after another until the fire is blazing and he can see the light reflect off the walls of his tiny bunkhouse room. He warms his bare feet by the fire and rushes back to the comfort of his bed. When he realized what he had done, he begged Sally to forgive him, but she was angry now as well and blamed him for all kinds of things that had happened in their marriage that he'd almost forgotten. He covered his ears and whistled a tune, but he could still hear her voice, so he left the house. He stomped around the block twice, and when he came back inside to make a point, she was scowling at *The Jerry Springer Show* on TV. A couple was beating each other up on the screen and screaming obscenities while the audience clapped their hands and chanted, "Jer-ry. Jer-ry."

"How can you watch that low-life trash?" he asked her, totally forgetting the point he was going to make.

She turned her head and scowled at him, but it was more of a frown, as though it were a cold day that was warming up and the snow was turning to freezing rain. He frowned back at her. They threw daggers back and forth until finally he relented and said in a low whisper, "I'm sorry."

"Sorry for what?" she whispered back.

"Sorry for slapping you and pushing you on the sofa. I'll never do that again as long as I live."

"You better not," she whispered, "or I'll leave."

At Christmas, the Wells leave the ranch in his care for a week and fly east to visit Ross's parents in Philadelphia. They leave behind a number where Fred can call them and another one of the local ranchers who can help out if needed. All he has to do is feed the cattle and horses that had been herded together in the feedlots they built.

Fred moves his things into the two-story Colonial where Ross said he could stay and makes a bed out of a sofa near the furnace. He turns up the heat and calls Sally.

"Good to hear from you." She's sarcastic, he can tell. "I just love being alone for Christmas."

"Then why don't you move here? We could start all over."

"Are you kidding? I'm not insane."

There's an interminable silence on the phone until Sally says, "You're spending money."

"I know." They talk a few minutes more. Fred tells her how beautiful it is in Kansas, but she doesn't seem to care.

"Wake up," she says.

It takes Fred a couple of hours in the morning and evening to do his chores. The rest of the time he has to himself. One day he goes to Willard, parks his car on the main street, and walks through the residential part of town. He looks in the windows at the families—boys and girls, parents watching TV, playing. He looks at the Christmas tree with the different-colored lights that blink on and off, the lighted angel or star on top. Through one window, he sees an old couple holding hands. Behind them on a mantelpiece, he sees baby pictures, their children, no doubt. Could you tell if one of those babies was adopted or not? This was a thought that comes out of the blue.

Another day he visits the Manhattan shopping center to find a present for Sally for Christmas. He sits on a bench near Santa Claus and watches the kids whisper in his ear. One kid pulls on his beard. Another punches him in his fake belly. Santa laughs merrily. He checks out Santa's elf, a young lady in a red miniskirt trimmed in fur. When the kids thin out, the toothsome lady lights up a cigarette and leans against a column behind the Santa's chair. Fred wanders up to her.

"I'm a lonely cowboy," he says.

"That's not my problem." She blows smoke in his face.

That night, he gets drunk. He wanders around in the fields. It is windy. Clouds scud across the horizon and blot out the stars. He wanders over to talk to the cattle, climbs in the pen with the bull. The bull eyes him carefully, seems so immensely bored by his presence that he doesn't even turn in his direction, much less charge him. Fred comes to his senses long enough to scramble over the fence and collapse to the ground on the other side. He can't believe that he tried to pick up Santa's helper, though he wonders what it would feel like to lie next to her in his bunkhouse bed. Would she feel as warm as Sally, as comforting?

Fifi licks his face. He looks up at the sky. It's snowing. Fred wanders back to the house, the poodle at his heels.

He turns on the TV and switches the channels until he comes to a movie, a classic that he instantly recognizes. *Boys Town.* That's a queer thing to play around Christmas. They should be doing *Miracle on 34th Street* or that one with Jimmy Stewart that he and Sally like to watch, but *Boys Town*? Spencer Tracy is playing Father Flanagan saving the lives of poor, misguided orphan boys like sad-eyed Mickey Rooney. Boys, he thinks, running his finger along the peach fuzz under his chin. Boys. He sits on the sofa with his arm around the poodle and his mind on boys, baby boys and girls, for that matter. On the screen Father Flanagan says, "We are all God's children." Fred Putnam is not sure in what context he uses these words, but it's like a flash out of the blue again, Sally's very same words and now they mean something. Tears well up in his eyes. Fifi seems to notice and paws him sympathetically on the shoulder.

When the Wellses return from Philadelphia, Fred informs them that he has to leave.

"What the hell for? You barely started here."

"I've got a wife back east and we're going to adopt a kid."

"Then what the hell you doing out here?"

Fred shrugs. He feels like the biggest fool in the world.

"What I don't understand," says Ross, "is why every screwball in the country wants to work for me."

"Don't mind him," says Kitty. "Nobody likes ranch work anymore."

Fred gathers his belongings and puts them in the blue Vega.

Kitty and Ross saunter outside to shake his hand. He pats Sky on the shoulder and plants a kiss on Dawn's cheek. The billy goat hurtles around the side of the house and chases Fred to the Vega. They are all laughing and waving. He jumps in the car.

"You have a good life," Fred Putnam yells back at the Wellses as he slams the car in gear. He's intent on the road ahead.

The Heart-Shaped Box

WHEN I MET JUSTINE CLARK, I LIVED IN AN APARTMENT BE-
hind the Opera House on the first floor of a redbrick Sears
bungalow that had seen better days. The house sagged in
the middle. I could walk downhill from my bed at the Water
Street end of the house and uphill to the kitchen table on
the Opera House end where, outside the window, I could
see the entrance to the police station. The third room in
the house was the bathroom off the kitchen, a long, skinny
room with a sink and a tub. I painted the room black and
hung a black light. I painted the kitchen dark green and the
living room purple. The gas stove right next to my desk was
red, as was the smaller one in the bathroom. On the front
wall next to the door, I hung a western blanket and a Day-
Glo cow skull. I hung a picture of an Iroquois Indian over
my desk that once hung over my desk at home. The rest
of the pictures were psychedelic—Jim Morrison bent over
his microphone, Jimi Hendrix bent over his guitar, a field
of marijuana with the caption "This bud's for you." They
glowed in the black light that I hooked up with a timer to
my stereo. The light blinked on and off to the rhythm of
the music.

The reason I'm thinking of Justine Clark and the apartment behind the Opera House is that in the middle of the night, Cal Harris calls me from a bar in Manhattan, Kansas, to tell me that he and his wife of thirty years, Alice Eisenstadt, are getting divorced. Alice and Justine were best friends at Denison, so after I listen to Cal stumble through how depressed he is, I ask him if he's heard about Justine.

"Last I heard, she married an Irishman, and they're living in Dublin," he said. "That's seven or eight years ago. Alice lost track."

When I hang up the phone, I prop a couple of pillows behind my head and lie back. I check the clock. Three a.m. One of the bichons is whimpering under the bed. I feel like whimpering too, but I don't believe in self-pity. I think of Justine Clark instead, way before the Irishman, and I think of the past before and after I met Justine.

Before, I reached under the back seat of our station wagon when I was twelve years old, felt around for a schoolbook, and pulled out a red candy box in the shape of a heart. I opened the box, reached in, and felt something soft wrapped in red tissue paper, which turned out to be skimpy red ladies' panties and bra.

"Is this for you, Mom?" I showed her the box and its contents. I was grinning from ear to ear because, even at twelve, I knew what this meant.

"No," my mom snapped as she looked over the front seat. There were tears in her eyes. "Put that back where you found it."

My dad was the perfect father. Two months after I discovered the red box, he drove my brother and me on a cross-country trip to California for the purpose of male bonding. I remember one night we stayed in a lodge that stood on a pile of rocks that overlooked the Pacific Ocean. We were in the restaurant, and I was looking out a huge plate glass window at a fog bank rolling in. It was about thirty feet high and white as snow, like a bank of tundra inching toward us. The next morning, we climbed through this tundra to go fishing on the rocks. We used mussels for bait. Dad cracked the shell open, dug out the innards with a knife, and carefully wrapped it around the fishhook. He tossed the line in the water, and it was not long before the pole bowed and I reeled in a red snapper. Then my brother reeled in one. We landed eight red snappers. The chef at the lodge prepared our fish in a light batter drizzled in a sweet sauce. Normally I hated fish, but that night I ate everything I was served, even the vegetables.

My dad laughed. "This is what real men do," he said. "They hunt for their own food. They gut it. They cook it. They eat it. It always tastes better that way."

"We didn't gut it or cook it," said my brother.

"But it still tastes better," I said.

When we arrived home two weeks later, I found out what else "real men" do. They leave home, in this case, with a lady, the same lady whose gift I found in the heart-shaped box under the back seat of our station wagon.

A decade after I left my downhill nest that I shared with Justine Clark, I married my wife. She was a practical woman who didn't believe in "real men."

"You don't fall in love," she said. "You decide to fall in love."

We were married for seven years, at the end of which she wanted children.

"I don't think that's a good idea."

"I want three children," she said stridently, as if by raising her voice, she could convince me.

"No. Children are too much trouble," I said.

"You only say that because you think you're like your dad." Bev stamped her feet, but I refused to budge. She decided to divorce me and moved one state over, where she found a corporate attorney to marry. They have two sons and a daughter.

So I'm thinking of Justine Clark and what happened. I first set eyes on her at the truck stop on Route 70. Cal Harris sat at the counter, and I slid into a booth with Justine and two of her friends. The friends whispered about whose baby they wanted to have among the boys who sat at the counter with Cal. They were all theater majors except for Cal and me, who majored in English. Cal acted in plays, so I was the only outsider.

The friends asked Justine whose baby she wanted to have, and she shrugged. "No one's." She wore a long flowered dress and platform shoes she kicked against my shins a couple of times.

"Sorry," she said and smiled at me. She was glassy-eyed, distracted.

When we wandered out to the parking lot, Justine was the only one who offered to ride with me in the cab of my Datsun pickup while the others piled in the back.

I had just completed painting my downhill abode and wanted to put it to its proper use. So when I dropped everyone off, I asked her if she would like to visit my new apartment.

"No one at Denison lives in his own apartment."

"I do," I said.

"Wow." She tilted her head and looked at me inquiringly as though she were gauging my intentions. A strand of long blond hair covered one of her eyes; the other shined glassily like the surface of a frozen lake. She was stoned.

"Sure," she said. "I'll visit you for a while."

We drove downhill and parked on Water. Across South Main, the holy rollers were singing hymns and speaking wildly in tongues in the Grange Hall where they met every Saturday night. A cop was leaning up against the basement wall of the Opera House whistling "Amazing Grace" and practicing quick draws.

"Barney Fife," she said.

"Yeah."

I took her on a tour of the apartment. She liked the way the linoleum in the kitchen buckled.

"Like waves in the sea," she said. We sat down on the bed. I didn't try anything. I put a record on the stereo and turned it up loud to drown out the holy rollers. It was Donovan, "Mellow Yellow," I believe.

The lights flashed on and off. Blues, greens, yellows.

"Nice," she said.

I took her for a walk. The holy rollers were congregated out front of the Grange, talking. Some of them screeched off in their hot rods. The cop tipped his hat as we sauntered by. We headed up the street toward Broadway to the only traffic light in Granville. We sat up on a stone ledge in front of the Opera House and waited until all the cars were gone and silence settled in over the town like a wool blanket muffling all the sounds except for the click-click of the light as it changed.

"Sometimes that's the only noise in town," I said, "especially late at night. I can hear it from my porch."

She laughed. "You're crazy." Craziness was a desirable trait in those days.

We stood in the middle of the street below the light and looked down Broadway and Main. No traffic. You could see the reflection of the green light on the white walls of the Opera House. Then a click, and the wall turned yellow; another, it turned red. I leaned over and kissed Justine. We held the kiss until the light turned green again, and, in that time, I felt perfection. I wonder if Dad felt the same thing when he ran away with the woman whose present I found in the heart-shaped box.

I didn't see Justine for a month, and I didn't know what to think, though every night before I fell asleep, I thought of her. She was in a play, *Marat/Sade*, as Charlotte Corday, the revolutionary who stabs Marat while he's in the bathtub sponging his sores. After the last performance, instead of attending the cast party in the greenroom, she breezed into my apartment. We made love. I stared at her beautiful, washed-out gray eyes, and she stared back until those gray, perfect eyes went out of focus and her face softened. Across the street, the holy rollers were singing hymns. A police car raced down South Main, siren wailing. The red light coasted across the ceiling, blending in with the blinking lights timed to the music from the stereo. The music was the Cream's "Politician."

We filled the tub in the long, skinny bathroom and climbed in. The water made our skin glisten. The black light turned us purple. We melted down to our knees. We made the purple water roll violently like the ocean in a storm. The water splashed over the side of the tub. I was so caught up in the moment that I slipped in a puddle of water as I stumbled out to grab a towel. I crashed to the floor.

"Are you okay?" she asked, peering over the edge of the tub. I could see one of her purple breasts.

"Je t'aime," I said, leaning up on my elbow.

She laughed. "N'est-ce pas."

We went back to bed, fell asleep, and didn't awake until dawn. I had to sneak Justine in the dorm. She stayed long enough for the dorm monitors to see her and headed down the back steps of campus to Aladdin's, the local restaurant on Broadway, where I was waiting for her. It was Sunday.

We ordered brunch, but neither of us was hungry, so we picked at our spinach omelets until the Opera House opened. We went to the movies. *Zorba the Greek.* She put her hand on my knee. I whispered in her ear, "Bouboulina. My Bouboulina." In the apartment after the movie, we danced like Zorba to, I think, "White Rabbit," and collapsed on the bed. We took off our clothes. We made love on the bed and later on the kitchen table. The cop was outside the window, practicing his quick draw.

"Barney Fife," I said.

Justine Clark laughed. "I need to go. I mean, if I keep this up, I'll flunk out of college."

"I'll walk you to the dorm."

"No," she said as she was getting back in her clothes. "I need to think."

"Okay." I followed her to the door. She opened it, walked slowly across the porch, lost in thought, and down the steps. She turned. "I love you too," she said.

I DIDN'T KNOW what to think of Justine Clark. I didn't know what to think of love. I hadn't had much experience with long-term relationships except secondhand. But what the hell, I decided. When Justine dropped hints about her lack of plans for the summer, I dropped hints about how she could stay with me. We found jobs. The students left for vacation, the professors to study in Europe. We watched the holy rollers on Saturday night and greeted the townspeople when we went shopping on

Broadway. But we were basically all alone, with only ourselves to rely on. That may have been a mistake.

One night, six weeks into our sojourn, we hopped in the Datsun and tooled down the tree-lined back roads to Newark to sip a couple of beers at the Eleventh Street Market. We wandered around the square with the hewed-stone, gingerbread county seat building in the middle, the cars parked parallel around the side. The locals ran in and out of the shops. I felt a deep well of loneliness inside me, I suspect because this wasn't my town. Or maybe it was that my feelings for Justine were reaching a climax. It wasn't exactly the sex but that we were moving on to another level that I didn't exactly like. I sensed she shared my feelings. We wandered home like whipped dogs. We leaned back in our chairs on the front porch, staring out at South Main and listening carefully for the click-click of the traffic light as it changed. Justine Clark proceeded to guzzle the lion's share of a fifth of Jack Daniel's.

"You know the most important thing I want in my life?" said Justine, hooking the Jack Daniel's between her thumb and forefinger. "I want a baby."

"You're kidding." I took the bottle from her. I thought she wanted no one's baby, but, of course, she said that before she met me.

"But I want to wait. I want to go to the drugstore in Hollywood, where I'll be discovered like Lana Turner. Then, after I'm discovered, I'll take a screen test, and they'll cast me in a movie as the sister of the lead in a romantic comedy by Peter Bogdanovich. By the time I'm thirty-two, I'll have dozens of credits, quality ones, like leading lady in a Hitchcock film. You know those leading ladies. They're so sophisticated," she said in her husky voice and nearly tipped over the chair. "But it would all be meaningless because I didn't have a child. I wouldn't have anyone to share my accomplishments with."

"How about a husband or boyfriend?" I passed the bottle back to her.

"That's not the same. Boyfriends come and go, even husbands in Hollywood, but not a child. They're with you forever. Even when they're grown up and gone, they're still with you." I could tell she was on the teary side of drunk.

"Are you okay?" I asked her.

"No," she said, pushing herself up from her chair. "I have to go to the bathroom." She staggered sideways and nearly toppled down the front steps. I caught her, put my arm around her waist, and guided her through the kitchen. I waited at the kitchen table for what seemed like hours until she staggered out. She put her arms around my neck and wouldn't let go even after she collapsed on the bed. She dragged me down with her.

"Please don't leave me," she murmured sleepily. I reached behind my neck and pried her fingers loose.

The next morning, Justine headed off to work at the theater department, but actually she headed to the bus station, where she purchased a ticket for the Columbus airport, and when she arrived at the airport, she purchased another ticket for Chicago, her hometown.

I DIDN'T SEE Justine Clark again until the fall and then from a distance, with Cal Harris, strolling across campus arm in arm like two lovers, eyes on each other, oblivious to their surroundings. I hated my buddy Cal, but that hate only lasted two weeks when I saw her again with Wynn Jackson, another theater major, and Cal whining to me, "You ruined her. She won't have sex."

Then I saw her with Alice Eisenstadt. I blocked their path.

"I want to talk to you."

"No," she said sharply. She walked faster. I had to skip sideways to keep up. Alice looked at me as though I were something nasty that floated up on the tide.

"I have a right to talk to you," I said. "I deserve an explanation."

She stopped, tilted her head, and looked at me inquiringly as though she were gauging my intentions. A strand of long hair covered her eyes, exactly like that night I first met her, though she wasn't stoned.

"You want me to stay?" asked Alice.

"No."

We sat down on a bench between Talbot and Barney Halls, old brick and stone edifices that were built in a previous century when Denison was a Baptist seminary. Below us we could see the town of Granville. The trees were turning colors. I could see the white steeple of the Baptist church, and across Broadway the silver dome of the Opera House, and, through a break in the trees, my own rickety redbrick

Sears abode. All these places reminded me of my relationship with Justine Clark, and I remember how weighed down I felt. I tried to take Justine's hand, but she wouldn't let me touch her.

"I left you because I wanted to go home. I needed money," she said. "I needed advice too."

"Why?"

"About what to do because I was pregnant. I went to Mexico City. I had an abortion." She brushed her hair from in front of her heart-stopping pale eyes and looked straight at me. "I'm sorry. I wanted to tell you. I tried the night before I left, you know, with all that stuff about how I wanted a Hollywood career and I wanted a baby, but I got drunk. I chickened out. I'm sorry."

I reached my hand out again, but she pushed it away.

"We never talked to each other," she said. "All we did was eat and drink and smoke dope and screw."

We sat there for an impossibly long moment, staring out at the fall plumage spread out before us like peacock feathers. Far off in the distance, I could see Route 70, a blue line on the horizon in front of the long line of brown hills. I could hear what I couldn't hear downhill, the whine of the semis, and I wanted to be out there on that road with the truckers, going somewhere. It was my turn to speak. I was glad she got an abortion, though I didn't know it at the time. I was glad she ran off to her parents instead of relying on me to tell her what the right thing to do was because I know what it would be, and I didn't want to be responsible. That's what I felt on the one hand, but on the other, I felt cheated for the very same reason. I felt angry with her, but I wasn't going to admit it. I watched those gray, washed-out eyes of hers, her head tilted as though she were gauging my intentions, and all I could say was, "Christ, this is amazing."

"Yes, it is." She stared at me intently like she was trying to look behind my eyes into my brain. I started to squirm like a child at church. "Don't you have anything else to say?"

"Yes." I said the first thing that came to my mind. "You did the right thing."

She looked down at her hands. "Yes, I suppose I did."

She stood up and looked off to the distance where Alice Eisenstadt was waiting for her in front of Barney. "Maybe we'll talk later."

I watched her walk slowly away. She was weaving like a drunk. She turned around once. Her eyes were glistening. I could see one tear rolling down her cheek, but I wasn't sure that it was for me.

I PULL THE pillows from behind my head and lie flat, hoping that sleep will catch up with me. The bichon is still whimpering under the bed. The girl, no doubt. Angel. The boy is Fluffy. He used to have a swagger in his walk, but now they are both creaky. They were Bev's babies. But when the divorce came through, she left them behind with me and the house to pursue her corporate lawyer. I don't blame her.

Finally I fall asleep. I have a nightmare. Justine Clark and I are on an ocean liner. She falls overboard, and I dive in to rescue her. I drag her to a raft. We climb in. Justine's teeth are chattering. Her skin is a pasty color and feels like ice. I take her clothes off. I take my clothes off. I wrap us in blankets and climb on top of her. After Justine and I revive from the exchange of our body warmth, we make love. The raft washes up on a sandy beach. In front of us is a huge cliff made out of volcanic rock. We follow a path up the cliff. There is a native hut and, behind it, a waterfall that spills into a pool like in the movie *South Pacific*. Bali Hai. I can almost hear the music.

We make love: in the hut, in the pool. Then Justine Clark, as if by magic, comes out of the waterfall carrying a baby in her arms or maybe a dog. Angel. I wake up.

It is light outside. The dogs are barking at the front door. I roll out of bed and look out the window. It's the garbage truck. The garbage men are rattling the cans. I pad through the hall to the bathroom, where I turn on the shower. I am living the good life. I am a stockbroker. I have a ton of money. I have a ton of clients. Some of those clients are widows on the youngish side, and though I'm tempted, I have standards. I don't feel the same way about the women I work with, nor the ones I meet in my travels or in the clubs I frequent.

I have been with many women. Two weeks ago, I broke up with Nancy. She lived with me for a year. Before that, there was Dale and Kathy and Danielle. I hardly remember what Bev looks like. It's been fourteen years. What I believe, what I told Cal Harris after he stumbled through how depressed he was, is that when you're finished with a woman or she's finished with you, whatever the case may be, you put her out of your mind forever.

Conowingo

Dinner

VIC IS ATTRACTED TO NANCY AT ONE OF WALT AND HARRIET'S couples-only parties at their new house in the suburbs. She's the only other single. Harriet and Walt don't believe in odd numbers. We want our guests to feel comfortable. Until Nancy, Vic felt the opposite.

"I grew up in Conowingo near the power plant," she says. "I wear sculptured nails, pluck my eyebrows, and tease my hair. There's not an honest thing about me." She's dressed in a pink waitress uniform and black flats.

"I moved to this area two years ago and found a job answering phones at a cable television firm. Now I'm a researcher. Next they'll make me vice president because the boss adores blonds."

"I'm sure he thinks you're smart too," says Vic.

"Perhaps, but he passed over other women who are as smart and more experienced but none of them are blond."

They spend most of the party on the back deck in the chill fall air while the other guests play charades before a blazing fire in the living room.

"I graduated from Sweet Briar College, a finishing school for Southern belles. I didn't fit in there," she says. "I majored in business."

"I'm a CPA," says Vic.

"You look like one." Vic assumes she refers to his wire-rim glasses and bow tie.

"Harriet and I met at Camp Chesapeake years ago. She thought I was daring. I tipped the sailboat over in the middle of the bay. Nearly drowned. I ran in front of the targets at the archery range during practice. Moments after my parents left on Family Day that summer, I set a pile of dirty socks on fire in my cabin. I breathed the smoke in deeply, slipped into unconsciousness, and was rudely awakened when they dragged me out."

She puts her hand on his knee. She wears about eight silver bracelets.

"I could've died."

The moon peers out from behind a cloud where it's hidden most of the night. In this light Nancy seems like a ghost out of the fifties. Doris Day as a truck-stop waitress. He takes her hand.

He tells her that he and Walt were roommates in college in the early nineties. In the summer, they rafted down the Snake River and rappelled El Capitan. When they graduated, they moved to Bourbon Street. All their possessions were stolen—his CD collection, Walt's desktop. They got into a bar fight.

"We decided to reform. Entered graduate school at the University of Maryland," says Vic, pleased at his openness. "Walt ended up marrying the principal's daughter at his first firm he worked for. I work for Bond Beebe, own a condo downtown in Adams Morgan, a Subaru, and membership in a sports club where I play racquetball. I travel for business. I guess I'm an average guy."

"Oh, come on, you don't expect me to believe that," counters Nancy. "There must be something unusual about you."

"Well," says Vic, deciding to take a dive into the unknown, "my dad didn't like it that I went to Maryland. He wanted me to get a law degree at Stanford, like him."

Nancy kisses Vic, her touch so feathery that he can barely feel the pressure on his lips. "I live on Carroll Avenue in Takoma Park, a few miles from here," she says.

Vic drives Nancy home. She invites him in, fixes him tea. They sit close together on a couch. "Do you hear anything?" she asks.

"No, I don't."

"Total silence is nice," she exclaims. "In Conowingo, where we lived on the side of a hill that overlooks the dam, day and night you'd hear either the water roar over the spillway or the low hum of the machinery. Got to the point where I heard it five miles off when I was at school."

Vic spends the night in a room with a half-open door, and after they make love, he studies Nancy's face, half in shadow like an eclipsed moon. He wonders what kind of person she really is.

"What are you thinking?" asks Nancy.

"Oh, nothing," he says.

"You can tell me," coaxes Nancy. "I want to hear about you."

So he tells her that he grew up in a ranch house in the foothills that overlooked Boulder, Colorado, and the plains.

"I could see all the way to Kansas."

He says that sometimes when he was in bed at night after all the lights were out and he could hear his father snoring, he'd want to slip into his clothes and creep down the hallway and out the back door. "I'd hike up the mountain over the Continental Divide, down the western slope across the valley to the Wasatch mountains, and down the other side to Bonneville Flats or whatever the desert's called there until I reached California."

Nancy laughs. "You sound as demented as me."

"That's my escape dream," says Vic. "I have another one where I hide up in the mountains in a cave because the Soviets have invaded and fenced in all the residents of Boulder. I vaguely remember a movie about this. *Red Dawn*, I think it's called. In my dream, I sneak down and rescue a girl and take her up to my cave."

"What do you do with her there?"

"You know." Vic shrugs.

"Yes," says Nancy, leaning up on her elbow, facing him in the bed so he can only see one of her tiny round breasts, the other's in shadow. "You could rescue me."

Lunch

Over lunch at the City Cafe, Vic insists that "Nancy may appear strange on the surface, but deep down she's a warm-hearted person."

Walt cuts into his mushroom crepe, more concerned about how busy he and Harriet were the day after the party searching for oak veneer end tables to match the couch they found at Ikea.

"I like Nancy an awful lot," says Vic.

"I wouldn't if I were you," says Walt. "By the way, did she tell you how she likes the silence?"

"Well, yes."

"You can't tell me that isn't weird."

"It's weird if you don't understand where she grew up."

"Okay, Vic, you can make excuses for her."

"I'm not making excuses, Walt. I like her."

"You shouldn't," said Walt, stabbing a piece of mushroom crepe and pointing it as his friend. The white sauce drips on the plate. "Her father ran away when she was a kid and, I think, it did something to her mind. Wait until she tells you about him. You'll see."

Dinner

Vic takes Nancy to dinner at Vidalia followed by a concert at the Kennedy Center. She wears a low-cut black cocktail dress with a satin belt and satin pumps, a veiled pillbox hat tilted smartly on her head. He takes her dancing at a fifties club. She's in pink pedal pushers, saddle shoes, and an oversized men's dress shirt, and chews gum the whole time.

"I'm not what I appear to be," she tells him. "Insanity runs in my family. My brother's in and out of an institution in California because he won't take his pills. My sister's been released from a place in New Jersey. She suffers from postpartum depression."

"I know about your father," says Vic gently.

"You do. He was an engineer. He helped design the power plant."

Vic invites her to his condo. She peers out his eighth-floor window at the Jefferson Memorial and, beyond that, the lights from Rosslyn that wink across the Potomac like a thousand pairs of sleepy eyes.

"This is wonderful," she says. "When I was twelve, my father took me to Washington to one of his conventions. He took me to dinner at the Mayflower, to a show at the National Theatre, and the Ice Capades. It was just Dad and me. One night he ordered room service and we sat in front of a window that was high up like this one overlooking the whole town. I liked that."

Vic wants to ask further questions about her father but decides not to. She seems so vulnerable standing by the window, hugging herself.

The next day he calls up Harriet. "Don't let Walt influence you. There's nothing wrong with Nancy that a relationship with a nice person like you can't cure."

Vic falls in love with Nancy when he takes her to a ski re-
sort in West Virginia, though he's not sure why. They don't
ski. They spend the whole weekend in an A-frame with a
huge thermo-glass window in the front that overlooks the
lodge and ski slopes. They watch videos and build huge fires
in the stone fireplace, which they stare at for hours on end.
On Saturday afternoon it snows, and Nancy goes out on the
porch in a cashmere sweater, her arms wrapped around her.
"What do you hear?" she asks.

Though Vic's in his down vest, he still feels cold. He sees
the skiers winding down the slopes, waiting in line for the
ski chairs, cars driving down the road and parking, people
wandering in and out of the lodge and ski shop. But they're
too far away.

"Nothing," he says, "I hear nothing."

"Nor do I. Isn't it nice?" The snow gets thicker, obscures
the view of the lodge.

That night as they curl up on the sleep sofa in front of
the fire, Vic tells Nancy about his family. "My parents got
divorced when I was ten years old. Mom moved to Seattle
with my older sister. I stayed in Boulder and visited Mom for
a month in the summer. Tanya would visit us for Christmas
every other year and during the summer."

"Did you miss your mother?"

"Yeah. She's not a bad person. She and Dad couldn't get
along."

"My parents couldn't get along either," says Nancy, crossing her legs and staring fixedly at the fire. An ember pops.

"Because Mom was always right. Always. So Dad found an engineering job in Nevada. We haven't heard from his since. He might be dead for all we know."

"I guess we share a lot in common," says Vic hesitantly.

"Except that you got to stay with your father," says Nancy. She stirs the fire with a stick, turns toward him. They kiss, then settle down to make love with a wild abandon that Vic has never experienced before.

In the morning he looks at her body, which is as white as the sheets on their bed. Her fingernails and toenails are painted purple; two of her silver bracelets have slid up her arm. She opens her eyes, which are like black coral so he can't distinguish the pupils, and she says simply, "I love you."

Lunch

"I'm busy all the time," says Walt as he picks at his seafood pasta primavera at the Devon Grill. On a paper napkin, he draws the layout of the bathroom they're remodeling in their home.

"We're going to have a Jacuzzi, skylights, a walk-in shower. Kohler fixtures. The best that money can buy."

"Walt, I'm crazy about Nancy. What do you think I ought to do?"

"Forget her. You need a sensible girl. I wouldn't have let Harriet introduce you if I knew you planned to get serious. "

Vic picks at his seafood nachos with cheese. Walt says that it's bad for him. All that cheese will raise your cholesterol level.

Dinner

In the spring, before one of Walt and Harriet's couples-only soirees, Vic and Nancy have their first fight. He confronts her about the mental state of her family.

"I want to know how you fit in the picture," he demands.

They are in his condo, and she is standing at the window, looking out at the Washington Monument with its one blinking red eye. Vic is worried. They have been going out for almost a year, and things are turning serious. He realizes the next step is to ask Nancy to marry him, and he needs to make the right decision.

"Do you want to know if I'm crazy like my sister and brother?" asks Nancy.

He can tell that she is agitated. Maybe he's pushing his luck.

"Well, I'm not sure if I suffer from postpartum depression since I have never had a baby. Nor do I think I'm like my brother. He has an eating disorder. And I don't mean anorexia or bulimia. He weighs over four hundred pounds. I weigh in at a hundred and ten. Maybe I'm bipolar. Maybe one moment I fly off to the moon like a rocket and the next

I sink to the bottom of the ocean like the *Titanic*. What do you think?" She laughs, flops in a chair, and swivels around so she's facing Vic.

"Or maybe you think I have a personality disorder," she says, her fathomless black coral eyes flashing at him. "Why else would I dress up like a waitress one night and a bob-bysoxer the next?"

"Please, Nancy. Don't get overwrought."

"Well, you want to know if I'm as crazy as everyone else in my family. You want to know if I'm worthy of you. That's what I think."

"Nancy, Nancy," he says in a calm voice. "You're worthy of me. It's not that. I want you to talk. I want you to unburden yourself."

"You're not my psychiatrist."

"I don't want to be your psychiatrist. I want to be your…" He can't get the word out, so he finds a convenient substitute: "…friend."

"Wow. Friend. Like Walt and Harriet. Just what I need."

Vic feels an ache in his chest brought on by the sarcasm of her remarks. How real she has become. This frightens him. He can't think of how to respond, so he says they're late for the party.

They trudge out to the Subaru. Drive to her apartment, where she changes into a black leotard. Black miniskirt. Black tights. Black makeup. He wonders what kind of statement she is trying to make and realizes how little he really knows about this woman. But this doesn't stop him from loving her. He senses that if he said the proper words, the heavy silence that has settled on them like an anvil would lift.

When they arrive at Walt and Harriet's bungalow in Chevy Chase, the party is in full swing on the back deck of their house where Walt's cooking baby back ribs over a mesquite fire. He wears a "Kiss the Chef" apron, asks them whether they care for martinis or gin and tonics, and hands them a party plate of smoked cheese and Vienna sausages. In the background, Glenn Miller plays "That Old Black Magic," two couples waltz, the rest are gathered in a semicircle around the grill—Tricia and Zeb, Ed and Laura, Mary and Gary, Ted and Donna.

"It's hard to believe, but you're the only unmarried couple here," says Harriet. "As a matter of fact, you're the only couple without children except for Walt and I. But guess what? We decided this morning to think about having children. Isn't that wonderful?" They congratulate her.

Walt takes them up to see the bathroom that is finished except for a hole in a corner of the room.

"They're bringing the Jacuzzi in on Monday." He talks about the weight of the tub, with and without water, bearing walls, copper tubing, waste pipes, valves, and fittings. "I'm fascinated by the inner workings of things."

When they go downstairs, the couples crowd around the dining room table. Vic and Nancy sit next to Tricia, who asks them if dating practices are still the same as when she was single. "I hear a lot of singles screen their dates through private clubs."

"Yeah," says Gary, who's on the other side of Tricia. "That's how I met my wife. We saw each other on the internet before we went out together. It cost us a bundle, but it was worth it in the end. Besides, I sold my membership to the guy who moved in after me at my group house."

"You lived in a group house?" says Walt, who sits across from them. "Gawd, I'd hate that. Labeling yogurt containers, negotiating for bedrooms."

Vic notices that Nancy downs one martini after another. She stares fixedly at her hands folded in her lap. "How are you feeling?" This is the first thing he has said to her all night, and he is feeling guilty.

"I need to go to the bathroom," she says, pushing her chair away from the table.

He wants to follow her but waits until dinner is over, and then he follows the guests into the living room. They play charades. Nancy has been gone for half an hour, and finally he can no longer stand it. He climbs the stairs and knocks on the bathroom door but doesn't get a response. He hears the water running, sniffling. He jiggles the door handle.

"Nancy, are you okay?" He waits a few more minutes. The sniffling stops as though she's holding her breath. The water still runs. He breaks down the door.

Nancy sits on the toilet with the lid down. Her wrists are turned up under the faucet, sliced open across the veins. The blood spills from her wounds, down her arms, where it drips to a pool of water in the sink that gradually turns darker red.

"Jesus H. Christ," says Walt, who barges in behind Vic. He turns to Harriet, who's behind him.

"Would you get everyone the hell out of here," he growls at her. "The party's ruined."

Hospital

Vic visits Nancy at the psychiatric ward at Shady Grove Medical Center, where she seems preoccupied by perspective.

"There are people here far worse off than I am that have been here five or six times. They are serious about suicide." She maintains if she were that way, she would've slit her wrists when there was no one around to save her. She wears a cashmere sweater and a skirt embroidered with flowers. She insists that she must go home to her mother. Vic agrees to take her after she's released to his custody.

They spend the night at her place packing.

"I'll miss my job," she says. She makes him promise to tell the boss that she's physically ill and won't return to work. She wraps her arms around herself tightly as though she's either cold or giving herself a hug. She's no longer the ghost of Donna Reed as a truck-stop waitress. She has let her hair grow long, stringy—she is now a dirty blonde, a sixties character, perhaps Lisa in *David and Lisa*.

"You know it's my turn now," she says. "It was my brother's and sister's before. Now it's my turn."

Dinner

They drive north through Baltimore where they pick up Route 1, the main road forty years ago that now passes through desolate country with broken-down motels and seedy wayside stands, until they come out at the dam on the Susquehanna River. In Conowingo, they take a two-lane blacktop road that cuts through a forest and opens out at the top of a cliff that overlooks the river. They pull in the driveway of a white clapboard house with green shutters and window boxes full of flowers. A woman in a white uniform greets them at the door.

"Mom's a nurse."

Vic helps carry the luggage inside. He stays for a spaghetti dinner that the mother serves on paper plates. "I'm so busy, I don't have the time to wash dishes," she says. "And with Nancy here, I'll be twice as busy."

"I'm sorry, Mom," says Nancy, picking at her food.

"Don't worry, darling," says the mom in a soothing, nurse-like voice. "We'll have a nice time together. Won't we, Vic?"

"I'm sure of it," says Vic, staring at his spaghetti and meatball with green pepper specks. He dips the Italian bread in olive oil and listens to the silence.

"Conowingo is the perfect place for you to be," says the mom. "It is so quiet and peaceful here in the woods…"

"Except for the dam," says Nancy.

"Oh, don't worry about that. Don't worry about anything. Everything will be fine if you do exactly as I tell you." She smooths her daughter's hair. "I'm the nurse, after all."

Nancy looks pleadingly at Vic. She seems to be shrinking like Alice in Wonderland trying to make herself small enough to fit through the door that is too small for her.

"I truly appreciate your taking care of my daughter," says the mother at last. She has the same pale skin as her daughter, but her eyes are gray. Blank like a dawn without sunlight. She takes him by the elbow and leads him to the front door. "But now," she says, "my daughter needs to be alone. She needs to heal."

"I understand," says Vic. "I have to get back to the office. It's tax season."

He shakes the mother's hand and thanks her for the meal. He leans down and pecks the daughter on the cheek.

On his way to the bridge over the Susquehanna, he comes to an overlook and parks. He wants to hear the water roar over the spillway or the hum of the machinery. He hears nothing, a still twilight with the sun setting upriver casting long, twisted shadows from the bushes that hang over the cliffs. He thinks about that perfect morning in the mountains when Nancy opened her fathomless black coral eyes and whispered, "I love you." He thinks of what Harriet said, that there was nothing wrong with Nancy that a relationship with Vic couldn't cure. For a moment, what he wants to do is forget the past, throw away his bow tie, drive his Subaru into the river, and, like his *Red Dawn* dream, sneak up to the house with the flowers in the window box, rescue Nancy, and take her to his cave far off in the mountains where no one can find them. Then he remembers what Walter said about how he needs a sensible girl. Without a glance back, Vic climbs in his car and drives across the bridge.

The Right Thing

TOMMY PICCARD AND I WERE BEST FRIENDS UNTIL I DID WHAT I now regret: turn him in. I did it because I was mad. One Sunday he stole my shoe. He jogged around the block, and when I caught up to him in front of my house, he tossed the shoe to Ned. I raced after Ned, and he tossed the shoe to John, who looked like he was about to hand it over to me when Tommy snatched it out of his hands. I ran up the stairs of my house and threw open the door. Dad was reading the paper in the living room.

"Close the door," he said. "The dog will get out."

I ran over to Dad.

"Close the door," he said again.

I ran over to the door, closed it, and raced back. I was out of breath, sweating. I told Dad what happened. He sighed, put down the paper, and strolled over to the window. The boys were gone. "How old are you?" he asked, turning his eyes slowly toward me.

"Twelve."

"You know what I did when I was twelve?"

I knew what he did because he told me a thousand times. "Beat up the neighborhood bully."

"Yes," he said. He was a tall, cadaverous man, balding, with brown eyes set deep in his head. It was hard to believe he could beat up anyone. "I beat him up. I didn't have a dad to depend on." His dad died when he was ten. He had an older brother. I had an older sister, but she was out with her latest boyfriend. I was on the verge of pleading when he cut me short.

"You defend yourself. Use your brains."

I guess that was what I was doing when I turned TP in even though he was not a bully. Ned was. I knew it was Ned who put him up to stealing my shoe. Tommy would do anything on a dare. One time we were racing our bikes down the steep slope of Macomb Street where we all lived, and Ned dared Tommy to jump the curb. He launched himself up in the air and landed on the front wheel. He couldn't turn the handlebar, so he flew mouth first off the bike into a metal fence. He chipped his front upper tooth. The dentist decided not to cap it until he was older and less active, so when Tommy smiled, which was often, he looked like the British comedian Terry-Thomas. Tommy could curl his tongue behind that chipped tooth and blow the most ear-piercing whistle that you could hear up and down Macomb, even when I was inside my house. He would blow it in the morning when he picked me up to go to our corners across the street from each other. We were patrol boys.

I think Ned was jealous of us. Ned, as I said, was the bully. It's lonely being a bully. It's hard to get close to anyone when you're beating them up all the time. Ned loved war. In his room, he had framed pictures of World War II planes: the German Messerschmitt, the British Spitfire, the American Hellcat. He loved war movies, and every week, when it came on, he watched *Victory at Sea* with his father, a nervous, small man with bulging eyes. But the thing I remember most was Ned had a huge collection of metal and plastic soldiers. We would line the soldiers up across from each other in the sitting room while the TV was on to a war movie and start shooting them down with rubber bands. Sometimes, if I decimated more of his soldiers than he did mine, he'd lift the rubber band and shoot me in the face. Once he hit me in the eye, and I had to wear a patch for a week.

When I went to Tommy's house, we played All-Star Baseball. Ned thought it was a "sissy" game. He preferred Gettysburg or Blitzkrieg. Or we traded baseball cards. Or if we were bored, Tommy did some of his tricks. He could roll his eyes up into his head. He could barf into a cup. He had a voluntary esophagus. He could make farting noises into the crook of his arm. He blew songs like the national anthem or the *William Tell Overture*, the theme to *The Lone Ranger*. He could imitate cartoon characters such as Elmer Fudd or Yosemite Sam. My favorite, though, was Donald Duck. He spent hours perfecting his voice, and he taught me how to do it. You collect saliva in the side of your mouth, squawk into it, and move your voice up and down to make words. Sometimes we'd pretend to be Mickey Mouse and Donald in conversation. Mickey's voice was high and squeaky. He was even-tempered. Donald was his antithesis. He'd lose his temper, jump up and down on his sailor hat, squawk unintelligibly, and raise his feathers in a fist. Donald would get in a bar fight and lose. Mickey would figure out how to win without getting into a bar fight. Both of us preferred Donald Duck because he seemed more like us.

I remember that after Dad told me to use my brains to defend myself, I wandered out on the front porch reluctantly and saw the boys disappear down the steps to the Macomb Street playground. Tommy was waving my shoe in the air.

I ran after them. They were at the end of the long cement walkway that skirted the basketball court, sipping water from the obelisk-shaped water fountain. When I caught up, TP ran off to the baseball field, throwing the shoe in the air. He ran the bases. I followed him. He slid into home and bobbled the shoe. I reached down to grab it, but Tommy grabbed my trouser legs and yanked. I fell backward, and the shoe flew up in the air. Tommy caught it. He ran to left field and down a hill to where the swings were located. I followed at a slow trot. He was the fastest kid in the neighborhood. I was flat-footed. There was no use trying to catch up to him. But when I topped the hill, I saw him at the end of the playground committing the worse offense of all. He was rubbing my shoe in a pile of dog shit. He caked the front and side of the shoe, picked up a calcified turd with a stick, and shoved it into the toe of my shoe and stirred it around.

"You asshole," I said when I caught up to him. "What are you doing?"

"I'm polishing your shoe," he said.

Ned and John, though still by the water fountain, were close enough to hear. They both laughed, but I could tell John didn't get any pleasure out of this. He was lowest in the pecking order. Ned could turn on him at any time.

"You want your shoe back," said Tommy. "Here."

He tossed it in my direction, and I stupidly caught it, which elicited another peal of laughter from Ned and John. I wiped my hands on the grass. TP ran up the hill to the water fountain where Ned slapped him on the back. He put his arm around his shoulder, and they headed down the cement walk, up the stairs, and down the street, John trailing behind them. I knew where they were headed—to John's house. He had a pool table in the basement. I was not invited.

I picked up the shoe with a stick and took it to the water fountain to clean it off. Some older kids were playing basketball, including Chuck, Tom's brother. One of them yelled at me, "What the hell you doing? We got to drink out of that fountain."

My back was to them. I didn't want them to see that there were tears in my eyes. I felt like a fool. I felt like a coward, though I don't think I was one. I'd gotten in fights before and beaten up kids. Once I punched John in the stomach, and he sprawled to the ground, unwilling to get up. Another time, a gang of kids threw pebbles at me. I was alone. I called them names. They challenged me to a fight, one at a time. I squashed one kid against a chain-link fence, holding him there until he said uncle. I threw the next kid into the pricker bushes, and he started crying. Then the biggest kid grabbed me from behind and pinned my arms. The other two, whom I'd beaten up, punched me in the face and stomach until I started seeing stars. An old lady from across the street yelled at them from her porch. The gang ran off. So I'm not a coward. I'm not a crybaby, as one of the older boys on the basketball court called me. I was simply stunned by Tommy Piccard's betrayal. I hated fighting in the same way John did. I was a small kid, not very athletic, but I had a strong desire to get even, Father's way. Mickey Mouse's way.

Chuck took pity on me. He said he saw what happened. He got a bag, and I put the shoe in. Later I heard that he beat the crap out of Tommy, not for altruistic reasons. It was the sibling rivalry. I should've been satisfied with that, but I wasn't. It was one thing for Ned to treat me this way, another for my best friend.

Tommy Piccard had a darker side to his character. We all did, but he went further because, like I said, he'd do anything on a dare. I was with him when he stole a *Playboy* from the magazine racks at Peoples Drug Store. It was Ned's idea because he wanted to see the pictures, but he didn't have enough money. We waited across Newark Street, sitting on the brick wall. We were lookouts. TP sat at the soda fountain sipping a cherry Coke. He leafed through a comic book. I noticed a clerk staring at him, but then a customer distracted the man. Tommy sauntered over to the rack. Replaced the comic and sauntered out of Peoples with a big grin on his face. He rushed across the street and unzipped his jacket partway. We could see the masthead and a well-endowed bunny-eared female from the chest up.

But then Tommy went too far when he shoplifted a couple of sports shirts and a camera at G. C. Murphy's. All over the store signs warned that "Shoplifters Will Be Prosecuted to the Full Extent of the Law."

So when the manager collared him with the merchandise, the police were called. They shackled him. They locked him in the holding cell on Albemarle Street until he was released to his long-suffering parents. His parents hired a lawyer. He appeared before a caseworker in a juvenile division of the DC family court.

The caseworker scolded TP but also stated that she thought his family was taking this seriously and that he didn't need to be held over for trial. She told him that the files on his case were closed unless he committed another offense of similar magnitude. If he did, they would throw the book at him.

I knew the trouble that Tommy was in, but it wasn't until he rubbed dog crap in my shoe that I acted upon it. The Monday morning after my humiliation, Tommy and I and the other patrol boys lined up in front of John Eaton Elementary. We stretched out our arms and put our hands on the shoulder of the boy in front of us to make sure we were arm's-length apart. We marched up Thirty-Fourth Street, the lieutenant named Sheldon Bart, a brownnoser we all hated, yelling cadence. The lieutenant yelled, "Left, face." Tommy turned right and stepped in the street.

"About-face," he yelled to Tommy.

We all about-faced, and he told us to halt. Tommy was grinning.

After Bart told TP to ignore the next order, he told the rest of us to about-face, and we all forward marched up the steps to the school. Bart opened the door. One of the acoustic tiles in the ceiling dropped on his head. He fell back into Tommy's arms, whimpering even though the tile was made of cardboard-like material. We rushed to the front hall. The tiles were dropping in huge, soggy globs to the floor. The janitors and a few of the male teachers were rushing about, trying to sweep up the mess. The walls were covered with a fine mist. Paint was peeling. At first, I thought a water pipe had burst—it had in our house like this—and then I looked at TP. He was brushing the tiny flecks of tile out of Sheldon's hair and grinning from ear to ear. It was at that moment that I realized he had something to do with this.

It took him until the next weekend to confess. He invited me up to his room after telling me he was no longer friends with Ned.

"He tried to beat me up, but I was too fast for him. I got away. So he beat up on John instead." He laughed and started blowing farts into the crook of his arm.

Then he turned to me and smiled. "You know it was me who made that mess in school," he bragged. He told me that last Sunday after church, he had wandered across the street when he noticed that the door to the industrial arts classroom was ajar. He made sure no one was watching and slipped in. TP wandered through the school, thinking about what to do, making sure he didn't get near any windows so someone would see him. He went in the girls' bathroom to see what it looked like. It looked like the boys', except there weren't any urinals. He stuffed toilet paper down the toilets and flushed them until they overflowed. He went in the classrooms but had to crawl on the floor because there were too many windows. So he went in the main office. The blinds were shut. He found a lockbox and pried it open. Inside was about eighty bucks, which he stole. He opened his closet, pulled back some clothes, and showed me six unopened cartons of Topps baseball cards and a new thirty-four-inch Ralph Kiner baseball bat to replace the old one he'd broken.

"That's how I used the money," he said. "Guess what else I found? Two pairs of panties in Mrs. Hygum's desk drawer."

She's the principal. A German lady who, it was rumored, was a soldier's widow, though I found it hard to believe she was the wife of anyone since she was dumpy, had a big nose, and wore glasses that distorted her eyes.

"What did you do with the panties?"

"I kept one and raised the other on the flagpole, but the janitors took it down before anyone saw. Except for Sunday I showed John. You want to see something?"

"What?" I asked.

He reached in the back of his closet and pulled out the panties. They were pink and huge and still had the price tag on them.

"That's disgusting," I said. After this, Tommy started tickling me, and I jumped around like I was full of Mexican jumping beans and by accident I elbowed him in the throat. This made him mad, and he went after me with his fists, slugging me a couple of times in the shoulder and then giving me a hard one in the gut so I doubled over and limped out of his room to my house. I didn't consult with my dad, who wasn't home anyway. I went up to my room and lay down on my bed.

Tommy Piccard didn't know that he created a monster. I was so fuming furious at my former friend that in order to keep myself from breaking out in spontaneous combustion, I told Mrs. Hygum.

"Congratulations, you did the right thing. And don't vorry dar-link," said Mrs. Hygum—she still had a bit of an accent, "I von't tell a soul."

When I saw Officer Kris, the crossing guard, later that day with another policeman walking down the sidewalk in front of the school to a patrol car, TP between them, eyes downcast, looking like a condemned criminal, I knew this was serious business. But I didn't know how serious until Tom vanished from the neighborhood.

This was when I began to think that perhaps I had gone too far. It's not like this was Tommy and my first fight. We'd always settled things before without anyone knowing, especially a grown-up. What I did was an act of a coward. I thought about this for weeks. I thought about my own skin, and then I looked around me and thought about other people's skins, such as Mr. and Mrs. Piccard. Usually I'd see Mr. Piccard puttering in his garden or playing ball with his kids or taking his daily constitutional up Macomb Street to Peoples to buy a magazine or to meet his wife at the flower shop where she worked part-time. He talked to everyone he came across on his walks, even the kids like me. He'd ask me what I thought of the latest Senators game or if I planned to play for Maggie's next spring—that was our local baseball team he coached. But now I didn't see him at all, except trudging home from work with a hangdog look on his face. Or Mrs. Piccard—I'd see her rocking on the front porch of her house, a faraway look in her eyes. Sometimes she'd look up and see me, and her expression would change to quizzical as if she were wondering, Is he the one who ratted on my boy? Maybe I was imagining it. Maybe it was the guilt that got hold of me, but it was hard to imagine that with Ned.

After TP vanished, Ned asked me if I was the one who turned him in.

"No." I looked at the ground. I was sweating.

"Well, it wasn't me, and it wasn't John," he said, smacking his fist in his palm. I could imagine the bone-crushing vibration of that smack against my jaw if he ever found out the truth.

"Maybe nobody ratted on Tommy. Maybe Mrs. Hygum found out by herself."

"Well, maybe she did, and maybe she didn't." He was still smacking his fist in his palm.

Then, two years after TP vanished, he reappeared on the front steps of his house, a spacey grin on his face as though his mind had wandered off to some pleasant place in the piney woods and couldn't get back. "They got me on drugs," he said in a low voice I could barely hear. "They think that if I'm on drugs, I will change. I don't know why I have to change."

I knew exactly what he meant. I knew who they were and why they wanted him to change.

YEARS LATER, WHEN I was on a ski trip with my wife and two teenagers in Park City, Utah, I ran into Tommy Piccard. He operated the lift. I knew it was my old friend because of the gap in his upper front tooth and the spacey grin on his face. I don't think he recognized me. Tommy had dropped out of high school and ran away from home. I heard from his older brother that he drifted from job to job, though he always spent the winter in the mountains. He loved to ski. He didn't have family, a child, or even a girlfriend. He was that far gone, Chuck told me.

Later I told Connie about Tommy and my part in his downfall. "You shouldn't blame yourself," she said, patting me on the shoulder, her way of consoling me. "If it wasn't you who turned him in, it would've been someone else."

Last Supper

We meet the two men at the International House of Pancakes on New Hampshire Avenue. We sit at a corner table sipping coffee.

They are not what we expect. Not big, burly young men; bar bouncers; or sheriff's deputies who guard prisoners and need the extra money. They are middle-aged family men. Frank, balding, wearing blue jeans and a polo shirt. Ralph, also in jeans, a checkered shirt, and a Chicago Cubs cap. He sports a bushy mustache and is the skinnier of the two. He's the boss.

He tells us he grew up in Chicago, but he loves the outdoors, so he moved to Idaho where he met his wife. They have four boys ranging in age from toddler to teenager. Frank has two toddlers. All of the kids are doing great.

I ask them if they come east often.

"All the time. Washington, New York, Atlanta. The big cities," says Ralph, adjusting his cap back on his head. He looks straight at me. "That's where the problems are."

"You're lucky."

"Yes, I suppose we are," says Frank, though I can tell by the way he rolls his eyes at his buddy he doesn't mean it. We're a couple of idiot parents.

Linda is squeezing my hand tightly like we're on a roller coaster and she's frightened, which isn't far from the truth. We've been on one for six months since Sean was expelled from Birch.

We get down to business. "We'll be in and out of there in fifteen minutes," says Ralph. He tells us that we must wake Sean up. They'll be directly behind us. We introduce them, and if he seems okay, we stay. But if he's angry, we leave.

I tell him that he might not be alone. "He has a girl-friend who sometimes sneaks in in the middle of the night."

"No problem," says Frank.

"And an adult male."

Ralph says they're worried about adult males. One of them slashed a colleague's throat.

"Our policy is to call the police if there's a man in your son's room. They'll haul him away, and we'll be free to take over."

I smile. The thought of them hauling off Rob Chalmers pleases me, though I wish they'd haul him off to jail and throw away the key. And while they're at it, haul away Karen and Jesse and a long list of other people Linda and I hate.

She lets go of my hand, and we sit there staring out at the rush hour traffic creeping slowly down New Hampshire. The sun is pouring through the window. I blink my eyes. I put on my sunglasses. I pull the envelope that contains the check out of my pocket and hand it to Ralph. We follow him and Frank outside IHOP. We stand by our car and shake hands.

"See you at five a.m."

SEAN CALLS ON his cell phone. He's on Fourteenth and Kennedy and wants me to drive him and his friends to Strikers, an upscale bowling alley in Bethesda. They don't have any money, so he wants me to set up a tab that I'll pay with my credit card.

"Okay, I'll do that," I say, though inside I feel like I'm about to explode from all the pressure that's building up. I know that tomorrow it will be over. But that's no solace to me. I'd rather have Sean the way he is now than no Sean at all. I must do this for the same reason that I must drive him to Strikers; that I have, for the past six months, driven him to wherever he wanted to go like I was a chauffeur and not his dad.

I yell upstairs to Linda to tell her where I'm going. She's getting Sean's older sister ready for a dance.

"You stay with him," she yells back.

"You know he won't want me to."

I hop in the van. I cannot see how our lives have been reduced to kicking our son out of his house, but what other choice do we have? We don't know what's happening, but it's bad, beyond grass. We found a container of Ritalin under his T-shirts in his bureau in the basement bedroom and a plastic bag of ground-up Adderall he claimed he sniffed, though it could've been cocaine as far as we knew. And also containers of prescription pills I looked up on the DEA website. And lately his mom and I noticed that he was sick.

It was the mononucleosis acting up, we thought. He'd only been over it since March, and the doctor says it stays with you for a year. He slept through the mornings. When he awoke, he was often sick to his stomach. He'd puke in the toilet. He didn't eat. Then he'd go out on his daily forays with Rob, Karen, and Jesse; come home at midnight; and collapse in bed.

I cross Military on Fourteenth, the sun low on the horizon, blinding me as I climb the hill. I'm thinking about how we begged Sean to quit this insane running around but he refused. "Why should I?" he asked. "It doesn't make any difference."

Linda and I know what he means. Sean was expelled from Birch School for selling three marijuana joints on campus grounds even though he insisted that was a lie. But it was his word against two other students. "Preppy girls that liked me," Sean insisted, "though I didn't like them back in the way they wanted." Birch was a private school. The headmaster could do whatever he wanted. He didn't like alpha males. That was Sean. So he erred in favor of the girls. He wrote us a one-sentence letter that said, "At this point, our level of trust in Sean is so low that we have a hard time in seeing how he could function successfully as a student at Birch."

"It doesn't make any difference," Sean said after he saw the letter. "Lie. Tell the truth. Run around. Stand still. It's always my fault."

I turn left on Kennedy and pull up to the bus stop. I roll down the window. A tall, cadaverous man rocking back and forth on his heels stares in at me. He has a wild look in his eyes. He is clucking to himself. There is a drug house nearby,

I suspect, because this is where I often pick up Sean and Rob, though Rob insists it's a transfer point on the bus line.

Chicken man sticks his head in the window. Rob pushes him aside and climbs in the back followed by Jesse and Karen. Sean slides in the front seat. He puts his Child of Bodom disk into the CD player and yells, "Strikers is eighteen and over tonight. We can't go."

I turn down the sound. "Jesse and Rob can," I say hopefully.

"Hey, Mr. Runnels. Listen," says Rob, leaning forward as I drive away. I can feel his rancid breath on my neck. "What day is this?"

"Saturday."

"Then let's go out to dinner," he says. "It's important that we celebrate."

"Celebrate what?" I hate Rob more than anyone else on earth, though I've only known him for two months. He's a down-and-out California surfer type—tanned, blond, blue eyes— though under the eyes are dark circles that give him a raccoon-like appearance. He wears long shirts. He's shivering even though it's 87 degrees out after the sun has set. I take off my sunglasses and put on my regular specs. Rob begs me to turn off the air conditioner and asks me what day it is again.

Sean waves at a dark-skinned man with black hair who is leaning against a telephone pole, smoking a cigarette.

"That's Rob's friend," he says.

The drug dealer, I'm thinking.

"Yeah, we're celebrating because he's renting me a room in his family's house." Rob's been looking for a place to rent ever since I've known him. His mother is selling the house and moving to California to be near Rob's sister.

"He's living there with his grandparents, his sister, and his Chihuahua. He has a pet Chihuahua that we step on all the time. Don't we, Sean." He punches him in the shoulder.

"Yeah." Sean bangs his hands against his knees in perfect rhythm to the Child of Bodom drummer. "Yeah, he's way smaller than Fluffy and Angel."

These are our two bichons. Sean loves those dogs, and they love him back. They sleep with him every night unless he has one of his friends over.

"Hey, girls," yells Rob. "Where do you want to go to dinner?"

"I know where," says Karen. She's been whispering to Jesse. They grew up about a block apart off of Military Road and have been friends since they were five years old. "We can have dinner at the Cheesecake Factory."

"That's a great idea," says Rob. "Hey, Mr. Runnels. Can you take us to the Cheesecake Factory?"

"I thought you didn't have any money."

"I have five hundred dollars in the bank, but I don't have an ATM card. I'll pay you back."

"That's all right, I'll treat you to dinner."

"Thank you, Daddy," says Rob. I laugh. He is probably closer to my age than Sean's. Jesse's mom said that he is thirty. When he started dating Jesse, she made him take an AIDS test and show her the results.

"He's a degenerate," Jesse's mom said.

I take a left on Military, drive past Connecticut to Wisconsin where I park. On the way down the street, I realize I've forgotten my credit card and tell the others who are strolling in front of me. They decide that they'll stay here and make reservations while I go back for the card, a half-hour trip each way. I don't want to do this. I want Sean in my sight all night considering what will happen to him at five a.m. tomorrow morning, but I don't want to raise their suspicions either. The whole secret to snatching a kid is to keep it a secret.

I hop in the van and retrace my route down Military. I don't feel stupid for forgetting my credit card: I feel angry. I used to have two credit cards. The first I canceled when I found out that five hundred dollars had been cashed on an ATM at Fourteenth and Kennedy. The other I keep hidden in my room in a book on the shelf behind the bed. The reason I do this is that two weeks ago, I found the credit card missing from my wallet. It was hidden beneath a box of tissues in my wife's bedside table. I called the credit card company, and they gave me the last three transactions: a Safeway, a CVS, and an electronics store, all in the Friendship area, near where Rob lived with his mom. Any normal parent would confront their child about this, but I suppose we aren't normal; we are the idiots that the family men from Idaho think we are.

I pull into our driveway and turn off the engine. Margie is making her way carefully down the front steps. She is in high heels and a strapless evening dress. She is leaning up against her boyfriend, Jason, I think, though it could be Sam. It's hard to tell. She goes through a boyfriend a week.

"Hi, Daddy," she says as I walk up the steps.

"Hi, honey," I reply. "Have a good time."

And to the unidentifiable young man, I say, "You take care of Margie."

"I promise, Mr. Runnels." I watch him escort her to his car and open the door. He pulls away from the curb and drives down the street at about five miles an hour until he comes to the hill and picks up speed. I laugh. This is my perfect child with her perfect boyfriend. What distinguishes them from Sean is that they are afraid. Well, maybe not the boyfriend, but Margie for sure, afraid that she won't please me. That's what she gets from her mother and me, a desire to please her elders. She is a straight-A student, a virgin, and plans to be one until she marries. Once she was attacked by a boy and kicked him in the crotch. She earned a reputation, and only the nicest of boys will go near her.

I head upstairs to the bedroom. Linda is sitting on the bed, covering her face. "I can't believe we're doing this," she sobs. "I can't believe we're betraying our son."

"We're not betraying him. We're getting him help." I sit down beside her, put my arm around her shoulder.

She shrugs me off. "You're no help," she says and turns toward me. "What are you doing here? You're supposed to be watching Sean."

"I'm taking them to dinner, but I left my credit card here." I go through the books on the shelf behind the bed and finally find it in my confirmation Bible. Right now, I tend toward gallows humor.

Linda dries her eyes. She puts on makeup.

"Hurry up," I say. She wants to come to the restaurant. This is the last time she will see her son, we figure, in a long, long time.

WE ARE ON the first floor of the Cheesecake Factory in a crowded bar. The hostess motions us upstairs where a waiter takes us to a table. The waiter is a tall man with a shaved head. He has a dish towel over his shoulder and carries a water pitcher. We follow him to a corner table by a large window that overlooks the traffic inching up and down Wisconsin Avenue. Across the street shoppers stop and stare in the windows of the shops at Mazza Gallerie. A group of Sean's stoner friends that I've seen him with at Friendship pour out the main entrance of Mazza, followed by a security guard. They're laughing.

The waiter pours water in our glasses. He asks us what we would like to drink.

"Wine all around," says Rob.

The waiter eyes Rob suspiciously.

"Well, I want wine. Red wine," says Rob in a chastised voice.

"We have Merlot and Cabernet Sauvignon."

He orders the Cabernet; Linda and I, the Merlot. The waiter returns with bread and the wine. Sean takes a piece of bread and dips it in my wine before I can stop him. He passes the bread down the table. Rob is next to me. On his far side are Karen and Jesse, whispering to each other as usual. Jesse wears a nose ring, a belly button ring, and thick eyeliner that makes her look Egyptian. She is dressed in black and is so thin and pale she could be a ghost. Karen is more substantial. She also wears black. Her hair is black, though it is mostly covered by a bandana. Her skin is rosy; her eyes are green, slanted like a cat's. Even her voice has a meowy ring to it that makes it hard to understand what she's saying. Jesse's voice is whiny. They are staring at me in a hard, penetrating way that makes me nervous. Maybe they are trying to read my mind.

Rob is telling Linda and me for about the fiftieth time what a high-class family he comes from. His grandfather was the judge who convicted John Gotti, the Teflon don. He had a home in Cleveland Park, the one Rob's mother is selling. He belonged to Kensington Country Club.

"He was a golfer," he says. He dips a piece of bread in his wine and sucks it. Sean sucks on his wine-soaked bread and dips it again, in his mother's wine this time.

The waiter comes up to take our orders. Karen and I order bang-bang chicken and shrimp, Linda and Jesse vegetarian Thai noodles, Sean pizza—he only orders pizzas—and Rob filet mignon and lobster tail and a Tequila Sunrise.

"My granddad had a ten handicap," says Rob when the Sunrise arrives.

"Did you play golf with him?" I ask, knowing that his grandfather probably spurned him.

"No, I don't play golf," he says, taking a sip of his drink. "But I understand you and Sean play."

"We did until recently."

"Maybe we should all play some day."

"Maybe we should," I say, knowing that this will be the last day forever that I will put up with Rob Chalmers. Suddenly I feel guilty. It will also be the last day I will put up with Sean Runnels for I don't know how long.

He is leaning over toward Karen. She is whispering in his ear, and he is feeding her his wine-soaked bread. They are laughing.

"Hey, Mom, Dad," says Sean, looking up. "You're not sending me away tomorrow morning. Karen says you're sending me away."

"We're not sending you away," I say.

"No, we're not, sweetheart," says Linda.

Sean frowns at his mother. "You see, Karen," he says. "They'd never send me away without my knowing."

"Maybe," meows Karen doubtfully.

"I may be going away in a couple of weeks to a wilderness program, but not until then. Isn't that right, Dad?"

"That's right," I say. I feel guilty for what we are about to do because I love Sean. I know he is a good kid. He's good-looking, resembles John Wayne—he inherited this from his grandfather on his mom's side—and knows it, though not in an egotistical way. He has a sense of humor. Sometimes he swaggers around the house, hitches up his pants, and calls everybody "pardner." The girls love him. They call him on his cell phone. I can hear them giggling in the background: Juliette, Laura, Lisa, Katie, Nicole, Rita Embers. It's difficult to keep track of them. In sixth grade, we had a birthday party for him, and when it was time for him to open presents, the girls pushed the boys aside and begged Sean, "Open mine first. Open mine first." He's humble about the attention.

"The reason girls like me," he insists, "is that I'm the only boy who'll go shopping with them."

He's smart too, like his grandfather who has a graduate degree in electrical engineering from MIT and forty-seven patents that have to do with leak-proof, high-precision valves that are used in chemistry labs and the oil industry. What makes me think that Sean will be all right is that his grandfather was a real screwup when he was a teenager. He used to hang around pool halls in the small town he was from in Ohio where he'd get drunk and get in fights. When his wife's best friend found out they were engaged, she said, "You're going to marry that thug?"

Rob is telling us about his latest prospects. "My mom found me a job as a sous chef at Kensington Country Club."

"What's a sous chef?" asks Karen.

"A sous chef does the sousing," answers Rob. He sniggers to himself and raises his third Tequila Sunrise to make a toast. "I want to thank Mommy and Daddy for taking us out to dinner, though it may be last dinner they take us out to for a long, long time if not—"

Jesse clamps her hand over his mouth. "Shut up, you big baboon," she says.

He rips her hand away and raises his to slap Jesse, but then notices us. "Sorry," he sniggers again, "family altercation."

"What do you mean by this is the last dinner?" asks Linda.

"He doesn't mean anything," says Sean, shaking his head as though he thinks his mom is nutty. "Maybe you're tired of taking us out to dinner."

"Yeah," says Rob.

I pay the bill for the tenth time, it seems, for Sean and these penniless friends. We head down the steps of the Cheesecake Factory to the car, the four of them laughing and trailing behind Linda and me. Sean asks us to drop Rob and Jesse off at Jesse's mom's apartment, a couple of miles beyond where we live. That's fine with me. I don't want him at my house, considering what is about to happen. But what worries me is that Karen begs Sean to go to the apartment.

"We'll have fun," she says. But he doesn't want to, so we drop them off. We drop Karen off at the Metro in Takoma Park, a few blocks from our home. I know that Sean will leave the basement door unlocked and she will sneak in as she has done in the past. But this night I will not bother them.

THE ALARM GOES off at four-thirty a.m. I climb out of bed and put on my clothes in about five minutes. I walk across the hall and close Margie's door. She didn't get in until one, so I know she will sleep through all of this. I brush my teeth and comb my flyaway hair. I barely look presentable. I creep downstairs. Behind me, I can hear Linda's feet clomp against the floor as she climbs into her jeans. She is whimpering like one of our bichons. I go to the front door and let myself out. I turn around and look in the window. Fluffy and Angel stare at me, their noses pressed against the glass.

I sit on the front steps waiting and thinking, trying to make myself feel better so I won't burst out in tears. What I'm thinking is of Linda's dad, who didn't get married until he was twenty-seven and lost three jobs before he was twenty-nine, or my own dad, for that matter, who my mom wouldn't marry until he decided between her and Jim Beam. It's a family tradition to screw up before becoming successful. Linda's dad's a millionaire. Mine owned a PR firm before he retired to Florida. Even my sister, who was kicked out of both private and public school, teaches anthropology at the University of Pennsylvania and is known for her work on Pompeii. She has written two books on the subject.

I glance up the street with a sense of dread at the few cars as they pass down the main thoroughfare, Ethan Allen. Finally one turns—a blue van coasts down the hill, pulls to the curb and douses the lights. Ralph climbs out the driver's side, still wearing his Cubs hat. He motions Frank to the basement door and follows me inside. We pick up Linda and the dogs as we tiptoe through the living room. Fluffy growls at Ralph. Angel jumps on him. I shove Angel away. She follows at a safe distance.

"Is the adult male downstairs?" Ralph whispers to me.

"I don't think so. Sean's girlfriend is, I think."

"You check."

I creep down the basement stairs. I can make out the outline of their forms on opposite ends of the couch. They're lying on their stomachs asleep. I check Sean's bedroom. No one is in there. I open the basement door and motion Frank in. He steps over the threshold and waits. I motion Ralph down the basement steps. He flicks on the lights.

The first thing I notice is that Karen is not wearing anything above her waist. I throw a blanket over her shoulders. Her eyes pop open. She looks like a deer caught in the headlights.

I go over to the other side of the couch and shake Sean by the shoulders until he wakes up.

"What...what," he says, rubbing his eyes.

"Sean, this is Frank and Ralph," I say as I was instructed. "They're going to take you to the wilderness program."

Frank is at the bedroom door. He points at Karen and then at the stairs. She grabs her shirt and shoes. She flees up the stairs to the first floor. I can hear the front door slam.

"What?" repeats Sean. "What's happening?"

"This is Frank and Ralph. They're going to take you to the wilderness program."

Sean's eyes snap open. He focuses them on me. "I can't go today," he says. "I have things to do and people to see."

Ralph hands Sean his red Dickies and Darkest Hour shirt, which were lying on the floor at his feet. "Get dressed," he says in a harsh voice.

"Where are his shoes?" Frank asks me.

I get them from his bedroom. Frank and Ralph take out the laces. They don't want him to run away.

"He looks fast."

"He is," I say, "the fastest kid on his soccer team."

When he is fully dressed, Frank puts a leash around his waist. Sean seems oblivious to this. He is looking up the stairs at Fluffy and Angel wagging their tails.

"You can't do this," he says. "You can't take me away from my dogs."

But before he can break loose, which he tries to do half-heartedly, they drag him through his room to the basement door. I stand at the doorway as they drag him down the driveway. He's looking back at the house as if he's trying to take it all in one last time. This house that's he lived in all his life. I can feel the tears come to my eyes.

"You want me to come down and say goodbye to you?" I yell to Sean. They're almost at the car.

He looks up at me with those narrow John Wayne eyes of his that the girls I know are crazy about and says, "I don't want you to say goodbye to me. I fucking hate you."

The Bees

WE DRAG THE SUITCASES UP A NARROW STREET IN PLAKA IN A hurry to catch the Olympia tour bus. I'm falling behind. Breathing hard. I know Jillian is angry with me because I don't have her stamina. She's forty-three. I'm fifty-nine.

We huff up the steps. Find a seat in the rear of the bus across the aisle from a young man: blond; bronze complexion; blue sparkling eyes; and a big, warm smile he directs at Jillian. She smiles back.

"You're American, aren't you?" she asks in her lilting low-country accent.

"No, Austrian, though I live in zee US. South Beach."

"Now isn't that a coincidence." She giggles. "We live in Naples, not two hours away."

"Yaw. Yaw," he agrees, nodding his head. "I have been zere. Very exclusive."

"We live in the most exclusive part. Port Royal."

I don't like it that Jillian brags about where we live, though I can't imagine what she'd say if I followed her advice a year ago when I sold my business: summer in the Hamptons; winter in West Palm. Christ, who in the hell does she think I am?

All my friends advised me not to marry her. She is a gold digger. She had been married three times before to rich older men who left her money. The son of the last man called my son and tried to warn me off. She'll take you for all you're worth.

"Don't worry, I can take care of myself," I told Aaron and my other friends, though I wasn't quite sure. I was a shrewd businessman, but in affairs of the heart, I did not have that much experience.

Jillian eased my worries. She told me that some people called her a gold digger. But she grew up poor. She struggled to survive.

"Is it so bad that I like the finer things in life?"

I could understand that since I, too, came from nothing. I like the finer things in life as well, and it's much easier for me, as a man, to attain them. So we married three years ago, and up to this moment I don't regret my decision.

I put my arm around her shoulder in a possessive way and look over at the Austrian though he doesn't perturb me at all. He's dressed in tight jeans. Blue loafers. A yellow sweater draped over his skin-tight white T-shirt. I know where he's coming from. Versace territory.

The bus rolls out, and the tour guide, Leda—a young, curly-haired lady with waiflike eyes—points out the sites, the Temple of Apollo and high up the hill, the Acropolis. I don't pay much attention to her because I've seen these places up close. I look at the storefronts as we whiz down the main street toward Piraeus. A lot of adult bookstores, I notice. The Greeks are a randy bunch, and how can you blame them with all the warm sun, green earth, and blue sky and ocean? It makes you want to take off your clothes and frolic in the woods or soak up the rays on the beach. I squeeze Jillian's shoulder and pull her toward me.

"Oh, you're such a cad, Larry," she says, slapping my leg. "You can't keep your hands off me."

"You're right, I can't. I'm insanely in love with you." This is true and I know why. She is a beautiful woman. Five foot five. Black hair. Hazel eyes. Curvy figure. Gruff personality. A lot like my first wife, Ellen. One time I was having an affair, and Ellen had one herself to let me know who was number one. You got to admire that spunk.

Our first stop on the bus tour is Corinth Canal. I rush across the road to the tourist kiosk and buy a bee scarf because Jillian loves bees. I've also gotten her a bee playing golf, a crystal bee pollinating a crystal flower, a clock in the shape of a beehive that buzzes on the hour, and a charm bracelet of gold bees with ruby eyes. On the way back with my newest prize, I'm nearly run over by a mini-truck because my eyes are on Jillian. She's staring down the chasm at the water funneling through the Corinth Canal talking to the blond man. I wander up. Show her the scarf.

"Oh, a bee scarf, how cute." She stuffs it in her purse. Introduces the man. Vladimir Witt.

"I invited him to visit us in Naples."

"Isn't that nice," I say, though I don't think it is. She is always inviting people to stay with us. She thinks my friends are too old. Stodgy.

At the Theatre of Epidaurus, we take pictures of each other and I meet Vlad's boyfriend, Ted, who looks like a young Richard Nixon. Hairy, ski-slope nose, bushy eyebrows, and shifty eyes that glower at Vlad when he pretends to cup Jillian's breasts. She slaps the hands away playfully. I wonder if maybe these guys are bisexual.

Back on the bus Leda tells us about a jewelry store run by an American woman in the Amalia Hotel where we're staying. That's exactly where we head when the bus pulls into the lot. The American shows Jillian a big gold rope necklace studded with diamonds. Looks like a noose around her neck. Twelve thousand euro. I wince. I point out a gold necklace and earring set: a gold bee on the stud of each earring, a string of gold bees on the chain, and at half the price. She tries it on almost shivering with excitement. The seven strands of gold leaf pour down her cleavage like a waterfall. The gold earrings dangle from her ears like miniature whips. She gasps, "Gorgeous."

I agree to buy the pieces and grab her hand. Drag her toward the restaurant, but she protests. "You go ahead," she says. "I want to change."

Vlad and Ted motion for me to sit down at their table. Jillian saunters in a few minutes later and sits beside me. Leans over and whispers in my ear, "I'm not wearing any underwear."

I reach under the table casually as if straightening my napkin and touch her knee, but I'm afraid to go any farther. Jillian giggles.

"You're such a sweet, sweet, sweet man," she whispers in my ear. Then out loud, she says, "Look at my gorgeous new jewelry." She points at the gold waterfall. Flips the earrings.

"I think that is a Lalaounis, is it not?" asks Vladimir Witt.

"It is," says Jillian. "That's what the American lady told us."

"Lalaounis is zee best gold jewelry designer in Greece, if not the world."

Jillian grabs my hand and pulls it under the table. I yank my hand away and blush five shades of red. I whisper in her ear, "Please."

"Oh, I'm sorry, darling," she whispers back. "I simply want you to get a preview of what you're getting later. You deserve it." She gives me a coquettish smile. Digs into her lettuce salad. Souvlaki. Stuffed grape leaves.

Sometimes Jillian makes me feel cheap.

"We own a store in South Beach," says the young Richard Nixon, eyeing us suspiciously as if he knows what's going on. "I'm in charge of the art. Vladimir is in charge of the jewelry."

They tell us they are on a buying trip. Already they purchased some art pieces. "And this stunning Lalaounis your husband buys for you," rhapsodizes Vladimir. "I will find for myself to add to our collection."

Jillian rubs my knee under the table. I try to keep a straight face. I don't know what happened, but when Ellen died, the floodgates opened. Gradually. I had always been a nice Catholic boy. A virgin when I married. My only indiscretion, the affair, to see what it was like to sleep with a woman who didn't lie flat on her back with a shirt on and legs together to have sex. I liked it, but it was unfamiliar territory. I didn't know if it had to do with love. I truly loved Ellen. She was the mother of our three children, a great mother, and a great cook. I still dream of her brandied plum pudding. She helped me build the business that I sold when Jillian came along five years after Ellen's demise.

"We need to go," I say to Vlad and Ted, who look at us curiously.

"What's the hurry, darling?" says Jillian when we get in the hotel room. She knows exactly what the hurry is, but the thing is, I'm not as capable as I used to be. When we were first married, I decided to take Viagra because I thought it could make up for our age difference. What happened is what they warned you against in their commercials. I got a hard-on that I couldn't get off. At the doctor's office, I held a newspaper in front of my crotch. I sat down and waited my turn. The other patients stared at me like they were trying to diagnose my problem, especially one old geezer who leaned over as though he were about to ask. If he'd done that, I would've slugged him in the mouth. That's the kind of guy I am.

The doctor gave me blood thinner and told me to stay off Viagra. So now I take supplements: ginseng, zinc, and such. I eat a lot of nuts and oysters. But it doesn't help that much.

We take off our clothes and flop on the bed. What happens next is embarrassing, so I don't want to get into it other than to say we did have sex.

The next morning, we sit in the front of the bus. Leda wants us to mingle with our fellow passengers. We talk to Diane and Fred, a supersized couple from Minnesota, Fred's arms covered in nautical tattoos, Diane's in red blotches. Newlyweds.

"Those fellows back there"—Fred points in the direction of Vlad and Ted, who are talking to two college students from Hanoi—"a couple of fags."

"Oh, I don't think that at all," says Jillian, waving at Vlad, who smiles back. "They're business partners on a buying trip. They own a store in Miami."

"Well, I don't know," says Fred. "I don't have anything against their persuasion. Unless they lay hands on me, then they better watch out." He slams his fist into his open hand.

"Fred's not the least bit prejudiced," says Diane, patting him on the shoulder. "Are you, Fred?"

We are penetrating deep into the Peloponnesian peninsula, up and down mountains on narrow, twisting roads. On our right, the pine and olive tree covered mountains rise steeply to the sky. On our left, they fall off to the Saronic Gulf. When we come off the mountains, we are in valleys covered in olive trees. On the eastern edge of the valley, villages cling to the cliffs, all white, against the sparkling blue water and sky.

We head west across a long valley to a cluster of treeless hills. Climb one of the hills and park in a lot surrounded by tourist kiosks, the ruins of the Mycenaean kingdom. Dates to 1100 BC, instructs Leda. We climb the hill along a cobblestone path. I pull out my digital camera. Snap a picture of Jillian at the Lion's Gate, two headless lionesses carved into a triangular rock. Vladimir Witt wanders up.

"I found on my computer those pieces of jewelry you wear last night," he says to Jillian, putting his arm around her casually. I don't like the way he's familiar with my wife, no matter what persuasion he is. Nor do I care that she is responsive. She has her hand on his chest. "Lalaounis, as I zaid. Copies of jewelry they find at a dig in Asia Minor. Ancient Troy, zey think, maybe worn by Helen herself. Who knows?"

"Can you imagine Helen of Troy? The face that launched a thousand ships."

"You could launch a thousand ships," says Vlad.

Jillian giggles.

I wake up in the night in a cold sweat. I am dreaming of Ellen. I turn to say something to Jillian. She is not there. No surprise. She's an insomniac. I climb out of bed. Check the bathroom. Not there either. I throw on clothes and pace up and down the corridors of the hotel. Another Amalia. I wander outside to the parking lot and up a hill. In the distance, I see the first gold glimmers of dawn on the horizon. I sigh and head back to the room. There is Jillian, lying in bed.

"Where have you been?" I ask her.

"You know me. I couldn't sleep, so I wandered outside to the terrace in the back of the hotel."

"Oh."

"Where have you been?"

"Looking for you."

"Oh, how sweet," she says, unbuckling my pants. She reaches in and yanks on my dick.

"No, I don't want to do that right now. I'm tired."

I lie in bed next to her. She is stark naked. A musky smell radiates from her body that makes me dizzy. I change my mind. We make love. I lie back. Fagged out. I think of my Ellen dream. In it, she reaches out imploringly, surrounded by an otherworldly aura that makes me shiver. I try to shake the image from my head. Focus on Jillian lying next to me and the rising anger twisting my insides. I'm not sure where it comes from.

The next morning Fred corners me at breakfast. "I don't want to bother you, buddy, but last night I wandered out to the back terrace and I saw your wife with that Vladimir fellow."

"Were they doing anything?"

"Talking. Holding hands. That other fellow who looks like Richard Nixon was with them."

We climb in the bus. Today we travel to Delphi. As we head north along the peninsula, crossing over the bridge that spans the Corinthian Sea to the mainland, I'm thinking of how I am probably nuts. I remember badgering Ellen to sleep with me. She would say she was too busy. What is more important than sex? I would counter. It's the closest two people can get together. Oh, bullshit, she'd tell me. You think with your dick. That is probably true because that's a major reason I married Jillian. Love, also, and that she'll take care of me in my old age.

At Delphi, Jillian holds hands with Vladimir Witt. Leans her head on his shoulder. Laughing. I follow Leda around. We climb the hill along a cobblestone walkway. We cannot reach the Temple of Apollo because it is closed due to rockslides. Half a dozen Germans are arguing with the guards. They want to go up no matter what the threat. I turn around. Check out the view. Below us are more ruins, many columns upright, some with marble crossbeams. Other columns toppled. Lying in a haphazard row. Chipped and broken. The only intact structure is the bank with the Greek letters over the door. In the distance beyond the ruins are the mountains and, in the valley thousands of feet below, an army of olive trees marching up the hill in our direction.

I wake up in the middle of the night in another Amalia in the town of Delphi below the ruins. Jillian is not in bed beside me. I decide that I won't search for her, the hell with the bitch. I try to fall to sleep, but it's impossible. I turn on the TV to a spaghetti Western dubbed in Greek. I turn off the sound. Watch Clint Eastwood blast every cowboy that comes into his sights. I fall asleep. Wake up at sunrise. Jillian is curled up in the bed as far away as she can get from me.

Fred corners me at breakfast. "You know those Vietnamese students. They had a room across from that Vladimir fellow. They saw your wife go in that room and the Richard Nixon fellow come out a few minutes later."

"What did they see after that?"

"Nothing."

"Why are you telling me this?"

"Thought you ought to know. I mean, if my wife was sneaking around like that, I'd sure want somebody to tell me."

"Thanks."

I sit next to Jillian the whole day, but hardly a word passes between us. It's killing me. We spend another night at another Amalia. It's like déjà vu all over again. A few months after Ellen and I ended our affairs, I asked her if she took off her shirt for her lover. She said she did. "And what happened?" I asked. "He kneaded my breasts. It made me feel like, I don't know, a piece of bread dough," she answered. She was trying to be funny, but I wasn't amused. I kept thinking of the lover's stubby-fingered hands despoiling my wife's breasts and other parts of her body, and it sent me into a fury. I feel the same fury now about Jillian and Vladimir.

I wake up in the middle of the night. Jillian is not beside me. I stay awake for hours devising ways of doing away with Vladimir Witt—shotgun, knife, chainsaw—until my stomach's churning. I fall asleep. I wake up at sunrise, and there is Jillian curled up in the bed as far away as she can get from me.

Fred tries to corner me, but I run away. We are at the foot of Meteora, a thousand-foot-high rock thrown down by the sky, ten or twenty millennia ago. We climb in the bus. Follow a long, twisting road to the top of the rock to visit a Greek Orthodox monastery. I trudge sullenly through the corridors of the monastery, a wooden structure hanging on the edge of the cliff. I'm getting angry. I don't see Jillian, but I know where she is. I browse through the monastery store. The nun eyes me like I'm a shoplifter. But all I am actually is a man with a broken heart.

I shuffle out on the porch. Below me down a short flight of stairs, Vladimir Witt kisses Jillian on the cheek as Ted snaps a picture. Jillian throws her head back. She laughs gleefully. She kisses Vlad on the mouth. A couple of monks look on disapprovingly. I try to remain calm. This must be sacred territory for the Greek Church. I don't want to spoil anything anymore than if I were at the Vatican.

But I can't help myself. I lumber down the stairs. I lunge at the wife stealer. He backs up against a rock. I take a few swings at him that he dodges. Then I punch him in the solar plexus. He doubles over and falls to the ground. I grab him by the shirt. Lift him to his feet. Drag him over to a wall about three feet high. On the other side of the wall is a drop-off of about seventy feet into a rock-filled ravine. It is amazing how lightweight he is, considering all the muscle mass on him. It would be nothing for me to lift him over the wall and watch his arms and legs flailing in midair before he is broken to pieces against the rocks below. But I hesitate. This gives Ted enough time to jump on my back. Tear at my hair and eyes. I back up—Vladimir still in my grip—and crush Ted against the rock behind me. He slides off my back and crumples to the ground. I throw Vladimir to the ground next to him. I'm breathing hard from all this exertion. I'm fifty-nine after all. I feel like I'm about to faint.

One of the monks comes up. Puts his arm around my shoulder. "This is not the way to settle your problems," he says in perfect English.

"I know, Father."

I look up at the crowd gathered on the stairs: the Vietnamese students plus an English and French couple, shock on their faces, and supersized Fred and his wife grinning. Leda rushes down the stairs. Grabs me by the shoulder. Thrusts me toward the bus. Jillian runs up beside me. Takes me by the hand. "Are you okay?"

I am still breathing hard, my face turning red.

"I'm fine. Couldn't be better," I say, pointing to the ground. "But I don't want you hanging around with those creeps anymore."

The creeps hug the ground, afraid that I might hurl them over the wall to their deaths. And I'm capable of it. I almost feel like I have superhuman strength. I nod at the monk.

"Go in peace, my son," he says. He's about half my age.

I turn on my heel. Grab Jillian's hand, and the two of us march down the stairs to the bus followed by the rest of the crowd.

We make two stops on the way to Athens: one for lunch, another at the statue of Spartan King Leonidas, hero of the Battle of Thermopylae. Jillian holds my hand, leans against my shoulder, and prattles on about how she wants to buy the gold bee pin with emerald eyes she saw in the Acropolis museum store. "It would match beautifully with my beautiful earrings and waterfall necklace by...how do you say his name?"

"Lalaounis."

"Yes. It would go beautifully because the Lalaounis have gold bees on them too," she says breathlessly in her lilting low-country voice that I love so much. I can easily picture her in the moonlight under a moss-covered oak.

"We'll go back?" she asks. "It's two days before we fly to Miami. We have time."

"Yes, we do," I say, then cup my hand under her chin. She looks up at me.

"You didn't sleep with that Vladimir, did you?"

"No, I didn't. I saw him several times wandering around the hotel at night. And once I went into his room. But we only talked. I swear to God. We're both insomniacs."

"They're bisexual, aren't they?"

"I don't know if they're bisexual, gay, straight, or transgender."

"You're telling me the truth."

"Yes, I am." Her eyes are welling up with tears.

I lean down and kiss her. "I love you, Jillian," I say.

"I love you, too, Larry." I kind of believe her.

Where I Want

I DECIDED A LONG TIME AGO THAT IF I CAN'T HAVE WHAT I want, I can at least live where I want. That would be Verde, New Mexico. If you're driving north in the mountains on State Highway 33 a mile before the "Welcome to Carson National Forest" sign, you come to a bend in the road. In front of you, you'll see a sturdy red wood bridge over a burbling, rock-strewn creek, and next to it a small Adirondack chair made out of the same wood, where the students huddle in the wintertime waiting for the Mora school district bus.

On the other side of the bridge is a dirt road that cuts through an aspen grove before it disappears into a dark forest of hemlocks, much like a dark forest in a child's fairy tale where the wolves are waiting to grab anyone who wanders off the path. It's a gauntlet you have to pass through before you wind up the mountain to Baldy Pass, a bare patch of land that gives you a 360-degree view, the edge of the world. All you can see are the mountains rising in the distance like humpback whales in a blue sea. Or sometimes you can see a black cloud in the distance and a jagged streak of lightning followed by a clap of thunder that bounces from one mountain to another until you are surrounded by thunder-claps. It's an exhilarating feeling to stand on this mountain, which I do about every morning after I run. I'm in the most god-awful wonderful shape.

Below me in the valley is the Rio Verde. It winds its way through the green fields and the town before it disappears in Baldy Canyon. I've run that canyon a half dozen times in a kayak and nearly killed myself every time. Once I broke my leg and the wife dragged me out of the kayak screaming. She fashioned a splint out of a couple pieces of wood, slung me over her shoulder, and hauled me up a rocky path to an outcropping halfway up the canyon. It took her about an hour. Then she lay me down gently and scurried up the rest of the path to find Ed, her lover at the time.

My life's been pretty rotten up to now, and that's why I want to live where I want. The reason it's so rotten is that I've been married too many times, two to be exact, less by one than my mother. I'll tell you the places I've lived grow-ing up. Vernal, Utah. Winnemucca, Nevada. San Francisco. Seattle. Cleveland. Philadelphia. I even lived in Germany. Mom's second husband was in the armed services. I have one sister. She's lived with a man, but she's never married. She doesn't have children and does not understand why I do.

"What?" she ponders. "You want to ruin another generation?"

I think the best wife I ever had was Verna. But I didn't trust her. I trust the woods. I trust the sky. I trust the moun-tains. I even trust the weather because when you see dark clouds in the distance, you know that bad weather may be headed in your direction. You never know with humans.

When I moved from Winnemucca to San Francisco after my mom divorced my dad, her first husband, my teacher Miss O'Grady took pity on me. She was a petite Irish lady with red hair, freckles, and a radiant smile that lit up the classroom. For the first time ever I didn't mind going to school until one day she asked me to stay after class. She was disturbed by my interaction with the other students, especially Freddy Pesky, one of the more popular kids whom I was trying to impress. Freddy asked me where my father was. I told him that he was a spy for the CIA. He could be in Moscow trying to infiltrate the KGB, or he could be running guns to the rebel forces in Nicaragua.

"David, you're a very good boy," said Miss O'Grady. She squeezed my hand. "I consider you my friend, and as your friend, I want to tell you that you're making a mistake."

"I am?" I scraped my chair closer to her. She smelled fresh, like the clover in Vernal, Utah.

"Yes, darling," she said in a tender voice that made my legs weak. "I know you're the new boy. You want everyone to like you, but they won't if you tell lies."

That night I dreamed the Russians dive-bombed our school. I rescued Miss O'Grady and held her in my arms.

Two days later she caught me telling Freddy that there was a black car outside my house twenty-four seven with a man in it whose job was to make sure that the KGB didn't kidnap Mom, my sister, and me.

"David," said Miss O'Grady. "You know what we talked about when I kept you after school?"

"Yes, ma'am."

"Then why are you telling stories to Freddy Pesky?" she asked in a scolding voice.

I turned three shades of red and muttered under my breath that I didn't know why, all the while watching Freddy's face light up with a smirk. I was found out. Freddy pushed me to the ground. He told all the classmates I was a liar. They laughed at me. I hated him. I hated them, but most of all, I hated Miss O'Grady, and I swore to God that I'd have nothing to do with another human being as long as I lived.

There were other times I felt this way. With my dad, who sent me birthday and Christmas presents for a couple of years after we left him in Winnemucca but never visited. I haven't seen him in thirty years. Or my mother, who swore we'd never leave any of the places we left. But she was always kind to me. My first wife wasn't kind. I don't want to talk about her.

But Verna was different, I thought. She had my mother's kindness without her wandering eye. Then she met Ed.

If you go down the other side of Baldy Pass on the dirt road, you pass through another dark forest of hemlock before you come to a clearing at the edge of town. In the middle of the clearing is a small hill on the top of which is a two-room hut. It reminds me of the woodsman's hut in *The Wizard of Oz*. That's where Ed lives. But he isn't a woodsman. He's a wolf.

Verde has two streets: Main, which starts at Ed's hut and ends at a bend of the Rio Verde where the Cattleman's Bar is located, and Water. That's where I live. I have two willows in my yard, two dogs, and six cats. In the winter, the cats sleep in the mudroom in a box on top of each other to keep warm. I love animals.

In the middle of town on the corner of Water and Main is the Baptist church. We all go there on Sunday mornings even though we aren't all Baptists. It's something to do. On Thursdays, the church turns into a movie theater, and once a month it's the town hall. Most of the time, though, for entertainment, we go to Cattleman's. That's where we first saw Ed eleven years ago when Verna and I were freshly married. She was six months pregnant and looked like a barrel, but that didn't bother Ed. He asked her to dance.

One of the things I thought after I broke my leg and Verna hauled me up a rocky path to an outcropping halfway up the canyon was that I was going to die and not from natural causes. I believed that at last they got me where they wanted me, out here in the wilderness three miles from town. Verna and Ed would sneak back several hours later and roll me off the outcropping. I'd dash my brains against the rocks below or drown in the water. My body'd shoot down the rapids to Angel Falls, where it would catch up in the hydraulics and spin like a top around and around for an eternity.

I was so frightened of this thought that I tried to think of anything else that would put my mind at ease, and what I thought was that maybe I was wrong. What proof did I have that Verna and Ed were lovers? He called her up at all hours and visited our house. They'd sit on the porch and talk nonsense. Sometimes he asked her to dance at Cattleman's. I saw them kiss, but that was under the mistletoe. Is this a love affair? Once I caught her sneaking home at one a.m. She said she lost track of time. She was talking with Ed and a friend, Molly, at his hut. I got mad. I grabbed our wedding picture and dashed it against the corner of our fireplace.

"Stop with the drama," she said. "I love you, not Ed."

I tried to keep this in my mind like a mantra. She loves me. She loves me. The funny thing about Verna is that she has red hair and freckles. She reminds me of Miss O'Grady, so it was hard for me not to view her with suspicion.

When I heard her and Ed clomping down the trail to rescue me, my heart climbed into my throat. They lifted me onto a canvas stretcher.

"Be careful," I whimpered. I closed my eyes and held tightly to the wooden bars as they inched up the trail. I decided to accept my fate, whatever it was. It took another hour, but finally we reached the top. They lowered me down gently on a soft spot of ground covered with pine boughs near the canyon lip. I leaned up on my elbow and stared down at the Rio Verde roiling through the canyon a few hundred feet below, a clean fall. I looked up at Ed and Verna. They both smiled.

"How you feeling, honey?" asked Verna.

They got at either end of the stretcher and lifted it up. I could feel myself rolling from side to side. I felt the pain in my leg where it was broken. I held the wooden bars. This is it, I was thinking. I closed my eyes and waited, but nothing happened. They turned away from the canyon and headed over the ridge to the town below.

It took Verna a year to gather up the nerve, but finally she and the kids moved to Las Vegas, forty miles southeast in the desert.

"You're the jealous type," she told me.

Ed didn't move with her. That was three years ago, and, as far as I know, Verna's a single mom who works the day shift at the Wonder Bread factory. I signed the divorce papers, but I'm not like my father. I visit the kids all the time. The girl's nine, the boy's eleven. He spends all his time at the local skate park. I tell him to keep his helmet on or he'll break his head. The girl, Lisa, looks like her mom, the same silky red hair and the same freckles. She breaks my heart.

Sometimes I don't want to stop when I make it up to Baldy Pass in the morning. I blow down the dirt road like the wind through the hemlock forest and the aspens. I pull up at the red wooden bridge. I lean against the rail. I look at the license plates of the cars as they round the bend. The cars could be from anywhere. Texas, Louisiana, Pennsylvania, Saskatchewan. I've been to all of those places and more. I like to travel, but right now I need to catch my breath. Marriage is hard. You can't trust it. But living in one place where you want to live is easy. All you got to do is stay put.

Everyone Worth Knowing

WE WAITED AT THE BAGGAGE CLAIM AT THE MARRAKECH airport for Raymond and Carmen Kiser. Ray was in a wheelchair. He had a heart condition and wore a patch while he was flying that made him dizzy. When an attendant in a yellow jacket wheeled him out through a set of swinging doors, he was rummaging through the carry-on in his lap. He pulled out a candy bar. Tore open the package. He munched around the edges of the bar and licked the chocolate that melted on his stubby fingers. Ray was a chubby man. He carried most of the weight in his belly. It stuck out in front of him like a medicine ball. It was probably as heavy. The rest of him was thinner, a broad back and thick, muscular arms and legs, though his head was big. He had blue eyes and thick glasses. He wore a Texas Longhorn hat on his head.

I should not criticize Ray for his looks. We were both old warriors. We both had wives who were younger, prettier, and smarter than us, but Ray was not as willing to admit it. I am an old literature teacher who likes to keep the peace.

We gathered our luggage and made our way through customs. On the other side, we checked out the cards that were held up by a cadre of young men and a few women in headscarves until we came upon "Kiser." Ray arranged the trip. We greeted the tall, dark-haired, beetle-browed man who held the sign. His name was Hassan Choukri.

"Choukri," I repeated doubtfully. I'm hard of hearing. "Are you by any chance related to a writer from Tangier named Mohamed Choukri?"

"Why, yes, I am," said Hassan, smiling brightly as he helped us with our luggage out to a cab. "He is my great-uncle. But how did you know of him?"

"I was a literature teacher, and one of the writers that I studied was Paul Bowles. He lived in Tangier and was a colleague of your great-uncle."

"Isn't it a small world," said Hassan as we climbed in the cab. It was a van that we had rented for the week, and we all easily fit. Hassan sat in the front with the driver, who spoke no English. He instructed him in Berber and Arabic. Ray and I sat in back and the ladies in the rear seat. They were consulting the guidebook.

Ray overheard me mention Paul Bowles, and he told Hassan a story that I heard a thousand times before: that he used to attend Andrea and Dick Simon's literary parties, and once he met Paul Bowles, and they had a long talk about Morocco. "He inspired me so much that once when Carmen and I were in Barcelona—she is a native of that town—we decided to visit Tangier. We were disappointed, I'm afraid. It's such a dirty city."

"Yes, it is, but they a cleaning it up," said Hassan, smiling

brightly though if I were Hassan I would have been stran-
gling Ray at this point.

Ray shrugged. He went on to mention other writers he
met at these parties such as Meyer Levin, Guy Endore, and
Grace Metalious. I never heard of these writers except for
the last one, who wrote *Peyton Place*. They were best sellers,
no doubt, and us literature teachers are too highfalutin to
know their likes.

We arrived at the hotel in the medina. Ray went up to
his room and changed to his bathing suit and bathrobe. He
took the elevator down to the hammams in the basement
for a steam bath. This is a ritual he goes through every time
he travels by air. He says the steam burns off all the medicine in his patch. Makes him less dizzy and ready to face the
day. When Ray was forty-two, he suffered a heart attack that
bent him double in the middle of Park Avenue near where
he worked. The doctors said if he were lucky, he would live
ten more years. Then Lipitor came on the market. He is
now sixty-four.

After Ray left for his steam bath, Hassan took the ladies
and me for a tour of the Saadian Tombs. Hassan told us
about the Saadi dynasty and the royalty buried under the
tiled floors, but what I remember most was his reply to my
question about the meaning of the expression *inshallah*, one
that I heard several times from both him and his driver.

"When I leave you tonight," he said as I snapped a picture of the chamber of twelve pillars where one of the six-
teenth-century sultan's sons is buried, "I will say, 'See you

tomorrow, *inshallah.*' That means 'God willing.' We must add these words to all the things we wish for in the future because it is doing God's will that concerns us as Sunnis. If God wills that I die in an automobile accident tonight, that is what will happen, and I will not see you tomorrow."

I remember this because I am not a religious person. I'm not an atheist. I'm more of an agnostic. The fact is, I'm not sure why anything happens or who is in charge of making whatever happens happen. The other reason I remember this is that the rest of our day was defined, in my mind, by these thoughts, especially in regard to my friend Raymond Kiser.

After a short tour of the Kasbah, we returned to our hotel to rest before dinner.

Our dinner was an early one before the sun set. We waited in the courtyard of the hotel in the medina for Hassan to show up. We were sipping Coke Zero and snacking almond finger cookies.

I made the mistake of asking Ray if the Simons who gave the literary parties were the very same Simons of Simon and Schuster, the book publishers. Ray, who seemed totally refreshed after his steam bath and was dressed in his favorite designer clothes, a Ralph Lauren green shirt, blue dinner jacket, and khakis—he still wore his Texas Longhorn cap—said, the very same Simons.

"I used to date their daughter, Carly," he said, brushing the cookie crumbs off his shirt and ordering more cookies and goat cheese croquettes.

"You'll ruin your appetite," said Carmen in a peeved voice. She had probably heard this story before.

"I'm fine. I'm fine," he said, patting his substantial girth. "There's enough room in here to store the Taj Mahal." He leaned toward me and covered his mouth so the ladies couldn't hear. "You know that song of Carly's 'You're So Vain'? She probably wrote that about me. Our relationship ended badly."

"I heard that," said Carmen, laughing. "You know, it's really true. He knew Carly Simon. Isn't it amazing." She thought the world of Ray Kiser and his connections, and he thought the world of her.

We have been traveling companions for ten years, since we met in Paris where Carmen was attending an OPEC meeting and Ray was recovering from an angioplasty operation. He was skinny back then, a poster child for heart disease control, until after his second operation he decided, What the heck. I only have a limited time on earth. Why not enjoy myself? I knew that Carmen did not like this decision, but Ray was stubborn. His heart attack changed everything. He had to quit his ad agency job in the middle of the Toyota campaign. "My triumph," he called it. Carmen decided that they should not have children since she was the main source of income. Ray was a frugal fellow. He managed to save a ton of money. It was not like they were poor. They moved to Toronto, where Carmen landed a midlevel job in the oil industry. She worked herself up to the top and retired as an executive, though she still sat on a number of boards to keep busy.

Hassan Choukri appeared in the courtyard dressed in a brown djellaba and a flat yellow hat. He carried a lantern to guide us to a restaurant called Baharat. He stood patiently by as Ray regaled us about the Majorelle, a botanical garden and estate once owned by Yves Saint Laurent and now open to the public. We were to visit tomorrow.

"Yves was a client of mine and a good friend. I was on a shoot for his company in Barcelona when I met Carmen. She was a swimsuit model," said Ray, smiling at his wife and patting her knee.

Carmen blushed. "Please, Raymond."

But Raymond elaborated more on his close relationship with the clothes designer and how he and Carmen visited Majorelle until Hassan finally interrupted.

"I am very impressed about how many important people you know, even in my country." He looked at his watch. "But I must admit, we are running late. I don't want us to lose our reservation."

"Of course, of course," said Ray, standing up with some difficulty. His knees were bad. We followed Hassan out of the hotel and entered the souk. We twisted and turned our way past the vendors in their makeshift stalls yelling for us to buy their wares. Ray stopped at a silver jewelry stall. He haggled the price of a necklace he liked down to seven hundred dirham and gave it to Carmen. Carmen thanked him and said we must hurry. She had read in the guide-book that the chef at Baharat was the best in Marrakech, but impatient.

The sunlight slanted through the wooden slates in the roof and turned the souk an eerie bluish-copper color. It was hard to find our way through the shadows and around the crowds, but at last we came to a narrow street packed more tightly: teenagers in blue jeans jabbering on their cell phones and bouncing off each other; older men in tennis shoes and hooded djellabas looking less like Berbers than medieval monks; and women enshrouded in black, a few in burkas that covered all but their eyes. But most were in European clothes and came in all shapes, sizes, and colors.

"We are a multicultural society, unlike the other Arab countries," said Hassan with a note of disdain in his voice. "We are more advanced. The mayor of Marrakech is a woman, and recently we passed a law that allows women to divorce men."

Motorbikes weaved in and out of the human traffic, horns blaring, and the occasional donkey cart trundled by, one of the carts piled high with mattresses tipping precariously in our direction, another in tanned leather on the way to the leather auction in the souk. Dana and Carmen followed Hassan, who waved his lantern from side to side to make way for the tourists. Then came Ray, who wobbled from side to side like a car with a flat. I ran up to my friend.

"You all right?"

"Fine, short of breath. Close quarters." He covered his ears. "Listen to the noise."

It was disconcerting to my finely tuned small-town ears, all this din mingled together like the crash of brass symbols in the *1812 Overture*. Set my teeth on edge. We came to a wooden door in the wall that Hassan unlatched. A guard on the other side greeted us as we stepped over the threshold. We found ourselves in a garden surrounded by palm and date trees, rosebushes, lilies, Lavandula, flowering cacti, and morning glory vines climbing the walls. In the middle of the garden along a tiled path a fountain spurted water in the air. It was so quiet that we could hear the coo of caged lovebirds and soft music that came from behind another set of doors that we entered to an elegant mosaic-tiled lobby of a hotel. Hassan bowed slightly and promised to return after the "repast."

We sat down at the first table inside the restaurant, a room lined with more dates, palms, and flowered vines climbing up the glass enclosures and overhanging the ceiling like a lush paradise. The tables were arranged around an orange and blue mosaic-tiled pool. We could still hear the lovebirds cooing in their cages and the soft, reedy Moroccan music played by a band at the other end of the pool. We ordered a Chardonnay and Syrah from the Siroua vineyard in Morocco, as Ahmed, our waiter, suggested. He was dressed in a fez, a dark-red frilled Moroccan jacket, baggy pants, and a shirt. We ordered prix fixe, endless amounts of Moroccan fare served from a silver tray with the help of an assistant.

First Ahmed poured the Chardonnay and served pastilla, spicy palm-sized meat, cheese, and vegetable pies. Ray corralled half of the pastilla as we discussed the anniversary of the *Challenger* disaster, a subject that he brought up because he knew Christa McAuliffe.

"I am famished tonight," he said, brushing the crumbs off his hands and asking for more pastilla. Carmen cautioned him about how he should go easy, and he glared at her before launching into how he attended Christa's wedding to Steven McAuliffe.

Ahmed poured the rest of the Chardonnay and opened the Syrah. He served the salad. Ray Kiser picked at the dried fruit in one salad and polished off the eggplant and tomato in the other. We discussed the upcoming primaries, and Ray informed us that he grew up with Donald Trump. They didn't live in the same town, but they belonged to the same country club. "He's a bully."

This was a story I heard from my buddy a hundred times, but still he elaborated about how Trump commandeered the boys at the country club to hunt for stray balls and then he'd sell the balls back to the golf shop and pay the boys twenty cents on the dollar. "That's how he runs his business. Could you imagine how he'll run the country if he's elected?

"You know a funny coincidence," he said as he shoveled the next course, chicken and lamb tagine on a pile of couscous. He tore off hunks of bastilla. Ahmed poured the Syrah. "A funny thing, you know, that writer you mentioned in the cab this morning that lived in Morocco, I forget his name..."

215

"Paul Bowles."

"He was also a musician. He was good friends with Aaron Copland, and as a matter of fact, it was Copland who introduced him to this country.

The funny coincidence, though, is that Aaron Copland was from Westchester County. I strolled up to him once in Tarrytown and shook his hand. 'I love your music,' I said. He thanked me and I said, 'Only problem is I have a tin ear.' I was a smart-aleck kid trying to impress my friend, one of the Rockefellers, Mike, I think, the one that vanished in the South American jungle," said my buddy, pointing a piece of bastilla in my direction. It was dripping shredded chicken and white sauce speckled with spices. Ray's stubby fingers were dusted in confectionary sugar.

I was losing my appetite and Ray his equilibrium. He wasn't normally this effusive about his connections. Nor did he usually eat with such gusto like a dog that doesn't know when to stop. Even Dana, who, like Carmen, was of foreign extraction—she was Norwegian—and didn't display her inner feelings, displayed them now. "Are you okay?" she asked.

"Fine, fine," growled Ray Kiser, waving his bastilla in her direction. Some of the shredded chicken and sauce splattered on the tablecloth.

"Darling, darling, calm yourself," said Carmen, patting his hand after he let the bastilla drop to the plate.

"I'm calm," he said, smiling weakly. "I am very sorry, Dana, if I sound overwrought. It must be the medicine. I don't think I entirely burned it off."

"That's perfectly okay," said Dana, patting his other hand.

Raymond Kiser ordered a bottle of champagne to go with dessert. While Ahmed poured the bubbly, his assistant handed out the dessert: mhencha, almond breakfast buns drenched in honey; milk bastilla, fried phyllo dough cookies layered in an almond, orange, and sweetened milk concoction; almond cookies; and almond ice cream. My friend went at the delicious concoctions with the same gusto as before as he continued to name names of the well-heeled in Westchester County as well as Pierre Trudeau in Canada and an oil magnate on the Board of Regents at the University of Texas where he had gone to school. He had been invited to one of their parties because he had given a substantial contribution to the annual fund.

But I thought his brain had really cracked when he reached back to his first memories of rushing into his dad's dentist office and staring up at a man he'd seen on TV before. "It was...it was..." We all stared at poor Ray because he was speaking loud enough to attract the attention of diners at other tables. "It was Soupy Sales."

"No, it was, it was...Pinky Lee," he started singing in an off-tune, scratchy voice, "Hello, it's me, my name is Pinky, argh-h-h-h..."

Raymond half stood, grabbed his left arm, and collapsed to the hard tile floor, dragging the tablecloth and its contents with him. His Texas Longhorn hat fell off his head. I jumped up from my seat, rushed over to my friend, and checked his pulse.

"Excusez-moi, monsieur," said a man in a business suit from another table. "Je suis un médecin."

The doctor bent down next to me. He said Ray knocked himself out when he hit the tile. "His pulse is still strong, but as a precautionary measure, we must transport him to a hospital," he said in perfect English.

He introduced himself as Doctor Talb and told us that we were in luck because he was a cardiologist. "You are Americans, I assume," he said, pointing at the Longhorn hat that he picked up and gave to me. "Not to worry. I studied at the UCLA medical school." He called for the ambulance on his cell phone.

WE WAITED IN a stark room in the hospital with only a few chairs and bare green walls. Far off through an open window, I could hear the call to prayer. It was still early evening, and while the sun had set, I could still see a streak of red sky on the horizon and the outline of a minaret. Carmen sat in one of the chairs, a stolid expression on her face like a mask as if she were preparing for the worst. Dana sat in another chair, wiping tears from her eyes. I sat next to her, holding her hand.

Hassan stood in front of us staring down at his lantern and then into our eyes. He seemed himself about to break out in tears.

An hour later Doctor Talb came out. He told us that Ray regained consciousness. He seemed fine except for a cut on his head when he hit the tile floor. They were doing tests and should know within a few hours if he was to return to the hotel. Carmen sighed in relief and a smile broke on her face like the sun rising. We all hugged each other, including Hassan, who seemed the happiest of us all.

An hour later Ray was pushed out in a wheelchair. He wore a bandage around his head, his Longhorn cap, and a meek expression in his eyes, one of which was black. The sun set on Carmen's face. The stolid expression returned.

"I'm sorry," he said in a soft voice we could barely hear.

They wheeled him down to the taxi, and we climbed in for the trip back to the hotel. On the way there, Ray started talking about the first time he traveled to Marrakech when he was a child. He stayed at La Mamounia hotel and met Winston Churchill. He was about to tell us the details when he looked at his wife, whose stolid expression froze him in mid-speech.

"Oh, never mind," he stammered finally. "It's not important."

Crossroads

I PADDLE DOWN THE RIVER IN A CANOE WHERE MY JUNIE appears to me, sometimes in a voice, sometimes in a vision.

One day I round the bend above the levee and see a tree across the river. A beautiful woman balances herself on the trunk. I don't recognize her, but I think she must be a harlot from the city because there are two men with her. One is helping her over the trunk; the other is on the other side waiting to receive her in the canoe. She falls toward the water. A branch rips off her halter top. I can see her naked breasts flopping in the morning air. The men recover the halter floating nearby. Hand it to her at the end of the paddle. She dresses underwater. They help her back in the canoe, laughing the whole time, and push the canoe the rest of the way through the gap between the water and the fallen tree, then paddle off, their laughter echoing against the banks of the river as they vanish around another bend.

I rub my eyes. I am stunned at this vision from Junie and wonder, What does it mean? I love Jesus with all my heart and ask him to take my hand and lead me forward. That's when it comes to me. I laugh like those men laughed knowing what they were about to get. I decide to go to the city and bang a harlot. But before I leave, I do some preaching at the levee like I always do, from Leon's song:

I got one foot on the Levee
And one foot in the grave
Trying to do my best for Jesus
But there's no one left to save.

I preach to the air. I think that one day the levee gives way, the floodwaters pour in, and you drown. No way you can stop it, government or no. You can't dam up the will of God. But I wonder, Is it my fault or the fault of the ones who need to be saved?

I hitchhike to the city to find out from the harlot.

The first thing she says to me is, "Why you wear all those black clothes? You a preacher?"

"Yes, ma'am," I say, shaking my head sadly. "A preacher and a sinner."

She giggles. "No sin in what comes natural," she says, "unless you're married."

"No, ma'am. My wife died five years ago."

"That's so very sad," she says, stripping to her undergarments. I take off the rest. We wrap ourselves around each other. She's like the oak tree. I'm like the ivy clinging to the bark. It's a mighty fine pleasure, and when it's over, I lie on my back smiling while she cleans up in the bathroom. I think about the last pleasure May gave me. She was a fine woman, inside and out. We was up on the levee having a picnic on that very spot I do my preaching. I saunter off to find liquid refreshment in the trunk of the car I once owned. When I saunter back, I can't see nobody. I panic; yell for May. She yells back. Her voice issues from the depths of hell. I peer down at the roaring water, the sluice the government designed to channel the river, and there I see daughter Junie slide down the slippery concrete levee and May slide after her, reaching out to grab her hand. The last I glimpse my darlings, they are clinging to each other.

When the harlot comes back from washing herself, I am crying.

"What's wrong?" she asks. "Wasn't I good enough?"

"No, ma'am, you was fine," I answer.

She puts out her hand, and I plunk down the greenbacks. I hitch back home, thinking the whole time that I am on the edge of a revelation. I'm thinking that since May and Junie were swallowed by the river, I been wandering in the desert like Jesus, only unlike him, I fell prey to the devil's temptation. I stayed clean for five years. Now I'm dirty. The world's a puzzle, but it's a puzzle you can fit together if you follow Jesus. The month after my darlings climbed the stairway to heaven, I met Leon and he sung me the song that I use on the levee. Then Leon lit out for five years until last week I seen him walking down a dusty dirt road with a guitar slung over his shoulder. I hail him. He stops and looks at me like I'm a total stranger, then smiles.

"Oh, yeah, Bobbie Lee," he says. "How you been all this time? You got over your sadness."

"No, no, I haven't. It stays with you always."

"Yeah, I know what you mean," says Leon.

"Where you been these past five years?" I ask, raising dust when I slap him affectionately on the back.

"I been up to Mississippi where I met these two fellows at the crossroads, one named Robert Johnson; the other a tall dark stranger. I don't know who that stranger was. He vanished, but afterwards Robert and me played music together. Then Robert died, and that's why I'm back here."

"Can you play music for me now?" I ask.

"I sure can," he says as we tramp off through the piney woods past the shacks. There's a whole colony of us weird river folk. There's a man lives up on a hill. I never seen him, but I hear he's as rich as blazes and mean as a junkyard dog. I step on the front porch of Leon's shack and wait while he fixes me a glass of sweet tea.

"I'll play now," he says, sitting down in a cane-back chair on the porch. I sit in the rocker. Sip the tea he hands me.

Leon lights into "Levee Prayer," the song he played five years ago, only now he is weighty with conviction. His voice is raw and smooth as rye whiskey. His guitar tweaks, whines, and hums in your ear like that harlot in the city. It makes you tap your feet and sigh with pleasure.

"Leon, you was a good player when I first seen you," I say as I rock back and forth in the rocker, sipping the sweet tea, "but now you are truly inspirational."

"Why, thank you. Thank you," he says as he leans forward and pats me on the knee. "You know, I don't know why

I come back here other than I was full of miseries over the death of my good buddy Robert Johnson. Then I caught you yesterday up on the levee preaching about sin and retribution and nobody to hear your words. It's like the Sermon on the Mount and everybody got nuked but Jesus."

"What are you getting at, Leon Jones?" I lean forward in the rocker with bated breath. I know what he's about to say.

"Well, I don't know," he says hesitantly because he doubts his luck. He strums the strings of his guitar nervously. "I think, if you don't mind my saying so, that we are both good at our jobs. The only thing we lack is an audience."

"You want to start a church."

"Yes."

I shake my head in disbelief. The puzzle fits together. I been wandering the desert for five years, and now I find my home. I give Leon Jones a big hug. We dance around his porch, and within a week we open our church that we call the Church of the Arc in the Woods because it fit in with my visions. Only we're poor and don't own a building. We own a sign that we move from my shack to Leon's every other Sunday. Nobody comes. They are at church in the city. We put us a sign near Roy's Grocery that says "Why Go to the City for Jesus? Find Him at Home." We paint an arrow pointing the direction. Nobody comes. Then we write under the arrow "Food for the Soul." The next morning, we find the sign in the dumpster. Roy tells us he put it there.

"I don't cotton to competition," he says.

Then we open the church on Saturday, and a tall dark fellow shows up, a stranger in these parts, who's looking for Roy's Grocery. We sit him down in the audience, about four rows of empty seats. Leon Jones plays "Levee Prayer" and an instrumental that moves at such a high rate of speed that my eyes bug out in disbelief.

"That's mighty fine playing," says the stranger when Leon finishes.

Then I stand up to preach, and the stranger falls asleep. We have to wake him up to show him the way to Roy's Grocery.

"Mighty fine," he says again to Leon, and puts his hand on my shoulder. "But, you, son, lack conviction."

The next week there's ten people in the congregation; the week after, ten more. Leon increases his repertoire to five songs. I decrease my preaching time. We hitch to the city because Leon has an idea. We hail a taxi and climb in. Next to us in the back seat is a mason jar full of white liquid.

"How many you want?" asks the taxi driver.

"We'll take five."

He leaves us off at the harlot's house and hands us a sack of what Leon calls communion wine. We visit the lady and a friend she invites over. Drink one of the mason jars and wake up the next morning with headaches. We hitch our way home. A fat man with a round pink face and stubby fingers picks us up. He points to the rich man's house on the hill. "That's me," he says.

"I hear tell you're as mean as a junkyard dog," I say.

"Not when l meet a poor man with a good idea," he says.

Next day, he's in the congregation that's grown to sixty-six folk. I look through the curtain we put in front of the door. I'm worried. This ain't at all like the church I had in mind.

Leon reassures me. "Son," he says—he's about ten years my senior, a wise fellow. "I hear tell there's churches pass out communion wine every week. That's what we should do, only two communions in one sitting. Then we pass out the collection basket because, you know, well-lubricated folks is generous folks."

I commence to think we're steering down the wrong path until something inside me catches fire. I stand up to preach, my eyes lit up like a freight train at night. I throw my arms out to embrace the flock. I sense that they're mine for the asking, and I light into what I know is true in my heart. I am a sinner of the worst kind. I hitched down to the city the other day and banged a harlot. I drank half a mason jar of hard liquor, nasty stuff that give me a headache. I tell them this isn't the first time and describe in detail the others. Then I deliver the coup de grâce, how Junie and May slipped down the levee in the water to drown. How my heart is full of sorrow; how, in order to forget that sorrow, I sinned. Before I only caught the men. They jump and scream to me, "Go, brother. Go, brother." Now the ladies commence to blubber and rock in their chairs. That's all I got to say, so I look at the folks a long moment, sigh, and sit down heavily in the cane-back chair. There ain't a dry eye in the house. Leon lights into an instrumental.

When the service is over and the folks disperse, jabbering at each other in excitement, the rich man strolls up with his daughter. Shakes our hands.

"I got a proposition for you," he says, but I'm paying no attention to him. My eyes are on the daughter. She is the beautiful woman who was balancing herself on the trunk of the tree in the middle of the river that I mistook for a harlot. I think of her naked breasts flopping in the morning air and how I want to fondle them, and then I think about the vision. God works in mysterious ways, I think to myself. Maybe the vision Junie gave me ain't what it appears to be. Maybe the puzzle ain't fully fit together.

The daughter's name is April, and I find this mighty suspicious. There ain't nothing in the world ain't planned. April's father is rubbing his hands together as he speaks to us about building a church at his own cost if we split the proceeds from the services, 51 to 49. "Of course, I'm the fifty-one, and what I says goes." He smiles, showing his tiny, sharp teeth. I shiver at accepting his proposition, but then I am tempted by April, who seems as pretty as an angel from heaven, such white skin like the first flowers of springtime and blue eyes, like the color of the sky after the storm passes. I want her, and the way she looks at me, the feeling is mutual.

But maybe I'm wrong. It takes two months to rope her in because she thinks we're different. "I'm an educated lady. You're a hillbilly," she says.

"What are you talking about? The only hill around here is the one your daddy lives on," I object, my feelings hurt.

Every Friday, we drive to the city in her sports car to see a highbrow movie. The only one I like is Japanese, about warriors that help out villagers attacked by bandits. It's a long one, but gives me plenty of chances to hug and kiss her even though she seems reluctant.

"I don't like to make out in theaters. Only teenagers do that," she says on the way home.

"Then we can find us a motel room," I say.

"Please, I'm not that type of woman."

I scratch my head and tell her about how I saw her up by the river with two men. "If you ain't that type of woman, how come you was with them fellows?"

"They're friends from the university. They're gay."

"You're darn right they're gay. They couldn't wait to get you around the bend of the river so they could bang you."

"I didn't mean that kind of gay. I mean they're homosexuals."

"Oh, I understand." I take off my black preacher's hat and scratch my head again. "Homosexuals are an abomination to God."

"You see what I mean," she says, slapping the steering wheel. "I'm educated. You're not."

But she ain't as smart as she thinks because later I seduce her in the woods near the levee. She cries afterward. I feel like the worst kind of sinner.

But it improves my preaching. One thing I try is what Leon said in his song about the good book in his right hand and a gun in his left. Only my gun is a cap. I slap it on the lectern along with the book and commence to preach. When I come to a particularly important point, I lift the cap gun in the air and fire away. This gets the men to jumping, especially the ones that been asleep. Leon thinks this is a nice touch. He's writing songs like crazy. Never been this inspired, he tells me. We buy us a jalopy because we're raking in the money and drive down to the city to do us some research banging harlots. Nothing like sinning to inspire you, we both agree. And it's double-dipping for me because at the same time I'm banging away in the city, I'm sweet-talking April, and the guilt is building like a mountain so high I can barely glimpse the top.

This goes on for five years. After one, the rich man completes our church to my specifications in the shape of an arc, but it don't float like I want. Outside are two hot tubs we use as baptismal fonts. Inside we got us a front stage and cushioned chairs around tables to keep the flock happy. Off to the side we got us a long bar where we serve the communal wine. Leon invites his friends to sing with him. Some of the songs are raunchy, like "Tarreplane Blues," which is about more than cars, and "Big Boss Man," which cuts down the boss by saying, "You ain't so big, you're just tall, that's all." We even got us a gospel choir, and every Sunday we put on a gospel lunch. We are open Thursday to Sunday night, though I only preach on Saturday, like I used to. The rest of the time I tend bar, but I don't mind that. It gives me time for personal counseling.

By year three, I buy a Cadillac LaSalle. I bomb around town like I own it. Buy myself a dozen black suits, a diamond-studded stickpin, gold pinky ring, a fancy Rolex, and a house to store my goods. I invite April on vacations: St. Barts, Paris, and Santorini, where she almost jumps off the cliffs. "I love you so much," she says, "and I don't know why." I visit the harlots. I feel like I'm a big mouth gobbling down food, but it's Chinese. Five minutes later, I'm hungry again.

In year five a hurricane blows up the coast. Leon and I climb the rich man's hill. April's gone to the city to live with her gay friends. "I've sworn off the kind of man that bothers you at night," she says. "I'm lonely." It commences to rain. Leon thinks we should invite some harlots up and borrows my LaSalle. Drives off down the hill. The levee breaks and the water pours across the road, taking everything with it, including Leon and the car. I am devastated.

A few weeks later, I move to a government trailer. All the cash is gone, so I don't buy furniture. I sleep on the floor in the only clothes I own. I feel like I died and moved into another world, but I been to this world before. Folks ask me if we're going to build the church again. I say no. They ask me to preach. I preach, but it lacks conviction. I think on the levee and how it took all that I worked and prayed for. Not once, but twice. I'm having my doubts, but only for a moment, because one morning I paddle down the river. I come up to the tree where I saw April, and I'm not surprised that I see her again by the bank of the river, all alone. I'm thinking of why Jesus spoke in parables. I'm thinking of how all these years, I thought I knew how those puzzle pieces fit together. But I don't. I'm like a blind man in the dark room. Even if I switch on the light, I can't see.

Acknowledgments

ACKNOWLEDGMENT IS MADE TO THE FOLLOWING PUBLICA-
tions in which these stories appeared in somewhat different form: *Prick of the Spindle, Zone 3, Southern Humanities
Review, The Compass Rose, Weber Studies, Mary: A Journal of
New Writing, New South, North Dakota Quarterly, The Pinch,
Phantasmagoria Magazine, Karamu, Forge Journal, REAL,
The Broadkill Review, Sukoon,* and *Stress City* (Paycock Press).
Grateful acknowledgment is made to the musicians whose
songs inspired the following stories: "Riding the Fences" inspired by the Eagles song "Desperado"; "Happiness" inspired
by John Prine's "All the Best"; "Crossroads" and "Cool Guitar"
inspired by Jimmy Thackery and the Drivers's "Levee Prayer"
and "Cool Guitars." And finally, to Tom Birkner for his *Fast
Food* painting, which informed my story "Fine Art."

Share Your Opinion

Did you enjoy *Everyone Worth Knowing*? Then please consider leaving a review on Goodreads, your personal blog, or wherever readers can be found. At Circuit Breaker Books, we value your opinion and appreciate when you share our books with others.

Go to circuitbreakerbooks.com for news and giveaways.

Jeff Richards is the author of *Open Country: A Civil War Novel in Stories* and the domestic noir novel *Lady Killer*. His fiction, essays, and cowboy poetry have appeared in over twenty-seven publications, including *Prick of the Spindle*, *Pinch*, *New South*, and *Southern Humanities Review*, and in five anthologies, including *Tales Out of School*; *Letters to J.D. Salinger*; and *Higher Education*, a college composition reader. A fan of blues music, he lives in Takoma Park, Maryland, with his wife and two dogs and travels often to Colorado, where his kids live.

CPSIA information can be obtained
at www.ICGtesting.com
Printed in the USA
JSHW030550160621
15942JS00002B/260

9 781953 639066